MW01113985

Born in Australia, Ali Niche has been an avid reader since childhood. Her love of reading gave her a love for other worlds and periods of time. She graduated from university with a degree in primary school teaching which only furthered her love of reading. When not writing, she can be found with a cup of hot chocolate reading or watching sci-fi/fantasy on TV. *Rome in Egypt* is her first novel.

For Mum and Dad,
You have always told me that if I put my mind to
something I will achieve whatever I want.
Love you always.

Ali Niche

ROME IN EGYPT

AUSTIN MACAULEY PUBLISHERS™

LONDON • CAMBRIDGE • NEW YORK • SHARJAH

Ordering Information
Quantity sales: Special discounts are available on quantity purchases by corporations, associations, and others. For details, contact the publisher at the address below.

Publisher's Cataloging-in-Publication data
Niche, Ali
Rome in Egypt

ISBN 9781685621278 (Paperback)
ISBN 9781685621285 (ePub e-book)

Library of Congress Control Number: 2023905121

www.austinmacauley.com/us

First Published 2023
Austin Macauley Publishers LLC
40 Wall Street, 33rd Floor, Suite 3302
New York, NY 10005
USA

mail-usa@austinmacauley.com
+1 (646) 5125767

Table of Contents

Prologue	9
Chapter 1	11
Chapter 2	15
Chapter 3	20
Chapter 4	26
Chapter 5	32
Chapter 6	37
Chapter 7	43
Chapter 8	47
Chapter 9	53
Chapter 10	56
Chapter 11	61
Chapter 12	65
Chapter 13	68
Chapter 14	74
Chapter 15	77

Chapter 16   **81**

Chapter 17   **88**

Chapter 18   **90**

Chapter 19   **94**

Chapter 20   **97**

Chapter 21   **101**

Chapter 22   **103**

Chapter 23   **109**

Chapter 24   **111**

Chapter 25   **114**

Prologue

Long ago, in ancient times, there lived a fair and just ruler. He was much loved by all his subjects.

He treated them as equals even though it was a belief that he was the incarnation of a God in human form. As such, the people believed the ruler should treat them as lower-class citizens.

The ruler, though also believing himself to be a God incarnate, thought that he was sent to the people of his country to help them prosper. But he could not do this with a firm hand like his predecessors.

He knew what a firm hand could do to the people. It was the reason for his ruling. Simply, his father had asked for too much, and his people revolted against him.

The present ruler had inherited the throne on his eighteenth birthday and was married by his nineteenth. Together he and his wife nurtured the people into a time of trade and prosperity.

The people rejoiced when news came of an heir to the throne. But it did not last.

As soon as the news that a healthy baby boy had been born, unfortunate news of the Queen's passing followed.

As the young prince grew under the ever-watchful eye of his father, it became clear to the people that he would be just like his father.

The people of the land were overflowing with joy.

And that is where our story begins, in the seventeenth year of the prince's life.

Chapter 1

Fear and desperation. They were the main feelings running rampant through her veins. The fear was so great it would have frozen her in place if not for the arrows and spears being thrown at her, hitting the sand and just missing her bare feet.

This girl, no older than sixteen, ran across the vast desert, her once glorious dress now in tatters. She screamed as the yelling behind her got closer, and an arrow grazed through her matted golden hair sending it into her teary sapphire eyes.

Suddenly, in the distance, through the haze of heat, she could see a village. From the sight of a large building, as big as the villas back home, she knew it was a village of importance. Hope had begun to override her fear. *They can help me*, she thought.

And, with that thought and newfound hope coursing through her veins, she ran faster along the sand dunes ignoring the shouting, arrows, and spears volleying from behind her. Even the screaming pain in her legs from running for so long did not deter her from reaching her goal.

Everything around her became a blur. She didn't notice herself entering the village until she was in its centre among the market stalls.

"Help me, please," she pleaded with one person she passed. But they stared at her in distrust and scurried along. "There are men chasing me." She spun around in circles trying to get someone to listen. "Please, you have to help me." She could not understand why no one would help her.

Suddenly a gentle hand was laid upon her elbow. She spun around to look at the person. But before she could utter a single sound, he put his finger to his lips in the common sign to be quiet. When he gently started to pull her toward an alley between two houses, she silently followed in hopes she would finally be safe.

Looking at her saviour, she would describe him as a guard. He had a cloth over the top of his head that flowed down the back of his neck to the shoulders. He had a simple cream cloth wrapped around his waist that went to his knees. In one hand, he held a spear, and at his hip was what she thought was supposed to be a sword, but it was shorter and curved like a sickle. If he was a guard like she thought he was, then he was different to the guards back home.

Lucky for her, the guards of this village worked in pairs, and they had seen the girl's pursuers. As one went to help the girl and get her out of sight, one had gone to inform their leader of what was going on.

The girl opened her mouth to ask her saviour a question. But before the first word could pass her lips, there was a commotion in the market behind her. Turning, she saw that her pursuers had entered the markets.

Instinctively, she took a step back and into the chest of the man behind her.

Her pursuers started asking the people around them if they had seen a girl running through the town. The villagers, now understanding why the girl was frantic, all responded that they hadn't.

She noticed that they were starting to get angry. She knew that they had seen her go in this direction.

To try and stop their wrath from being unleashed upon the unsuspecting villagers, she attempted to take a step forward. The guard gently grabbed her elbow and shook his head when she turned to him.

Yet another commotion behind her stopped a rant from leaving her mouth.

Her pursuers had been joined by two more men – both from the village if their attire was anything to go by. One was wearing the same clothes as the one behind her. So, she was led to believe he was also a guard. The other man was more regal looking. It was clear he was a high-class person from all the gold he was wearing; gold crown, gold rings, gold bracelets.

He clearly had authority in the village as his posture screamed power. His actions also spoke volumes. The girl could not understand what he was saying, but the tone of his voice and his gestures both indicated he was threatening her pursuers.

It was obvious that they were not going to take the regal man seriously. They argued back with a passion.

When the guard took a step forward, with what looked like manacles, they gave up and left the village market.

So, they were threatened with imprisonment, the girl thought as the guard followed her pursuers.

When the guard came back and gave the leader a nod, the guard who was still gently holding her guided her toward the two who had sent her pursuers away.

Standing in front of the person who was able to command the pursuers to leave the village was very daunting. She felt as though she was about to be in the same situation as they were.

Like when he spoke just before, as the words fell from his mouth, she did not understand what he was saying. But she could tell from the gentle tones of his voice that he was not going to send her away. Her confusion must have shown because he stopped speaking, gave a gentle sigh, and pointed to the palace behind him.

He was offering her a place to stay, even for a little while, that would be safe.

This confused her even more. This was not the same behaviour that other leaders had shown when visiting her family. They would not have offered a safe place to stay. They would have easily sent her away or sent her to the dungeon for trespassing.

But not being one to turn down a generous offer, especially in a rare case such as this, she nodded with a small smile and followed the leader and his entourage back to the palace.

Chapter 2

The room the girl was led to looked like much of the palace she had been guided through. The walls were made of stone, much different from the stones back home. Instead of small and medium rocks placed together to form rooms of a reasonable height, these were large stones that would not have easily been moved by one person. The stones were gold trimmed and had images of birds, leaves, people, and other things she could not describe.

The pillars that held up the high roof, that could have easily held two of the largest villas, had people printed on them. But what caught her attention were the heads on the people. They were the heads of animals. A cat, a lion, a jackal and many hawks.

She jumped when she heard a soft voice behind her saying, "That's the God Ra." She had been looking at the hawk-headed people, this one crowned with a solar disk and serpent, when another girl entered the room. "He's the supreme Sun God who travels across the sky during the day and the Underworld at night." This new girl was wearing a dress similar to the ones she had seen on the women in the village, one of rough-looking linen with feathers and simple beads sewn into it. On her feet were sandals made from what looked like reeds.

The girl was so shocked that the other could speak in her language she almost forgot she had a voice. "Who…" she squeaked. "Who are you?"

"Sorry," the other girl paused. "I'm Juliana. The Pharaoh asked me to help you get settled in." Juliana had her jade eyes turned down and was playing nervously with her black hair.

The girl instantly felt guilty. She walked toward Juliana and gently grabbed her hands. "Please don't do that," she said. "You don't need to be so formal with me." Juliana slowly looked up to see the small smile on the girl's face and smiled back. "Much better. My name is…" She paused. She couldn't exactly give them her real name, could she? "Ana." She thought it would be best to give them part of her name.

If Juliana noticed the pause, she didn't show it. "Ana," she giggled. "I like it." The two girls giggled for a few more minutes before Juliana remembered why she was in Ana's room in the first place. "A bath has been prepared for you."

"Thank you."

As the two walked down the halls to the bathing rooms, Ana couldn't help but ask, "If you can speak my language, how did you come to be here? You can't be any older than fifteen."

Juliana gave a small giggle. "I'm actually sixteen. I just look slightly younger than my age. My mother was the same. I was born in Rome. Just after my birth, my parents wanted to get away from all the politics, so they sold our small home and boarded a boat heading this way. They asked where the closest village to the port was, bought food and water, and started to walk. But they did not realize how hot the trek would be, and they slowly started to run out of water. Luckily, on the third day of walking, the Pharaoh himself and some guards were out for a ride to check the lands. They spotted us collapsed from exhaustion and lack of water. We were quickly brought to the palace, and the healer nursed us back to health. When he heard our story, the Pharaoh offered us a place to stay and work. I have grown up with the Egyptian language spoken around me, but my mother also wanted me to know our home language." She paused in remembrance of her years spent growing up in the palace. "He's offering you the same thing," she suddenly said, making Ana jump slightly.

"Pardon?" she asked.

"He has offered to let you stay in the palace until you want to move on. He's also offering you sanctuary if the ones chasing you come back again."

"That's awfully generous of him. He doesn't even know me."

Juliana simply shrugged her shoulders as if it was a common day occurrence. "What about you?" she asked. "What brings you from home to Egypt?"

Ana started. *What do I say?* She thought. *I can't tell them exactly what happened.* After having an internal battle with herself, she decided to tell Juliana the simple version. "I had some family issues I had to get away from." She said nothing more on the subject. With her eyes filled with tears and her head lowered in sorrow, she continued to follow Juliana through the halls.

No further conversation was made for the rest of the walk.

Soon Ana could smell the moisture in the air. But before they could reach the source, a male voice called from behind.

Juliana stopped and turned to answer. This made Ana stop as well.

The man who had called out could not have been much older than eighteen. His brown hair was long enough to just touch his shoulders and fell slightly into his forest green eyes. From the high-quality clothes and the small gold crown holding his hair back, Ana knew he was from the higher class and quite possibly the son of the Pharaoh.

The way he spoke to Juliana calmed her down slightly. Again, it was the opposite of how the higher class would speak to those in the lower classes. Instead of with a sneer and being demanding, he had a smile and amusement in his voice. It was another thing that caught her attention though.

With a nod and a smile, the man walked back down the hall the way they had come. Ana could not help but stare at him in shock and confusion as he walked away.

"Are you okay?" The question from Juliana pulled Ana from her staring, and she turned, blinking, to face the other girl. "What is it?"

"Who was that?" Ana asked.

"That was Ramses. He's Pharaoh Menes's son."

Ana nodded slowly, processing that small amount of information. She was right about who he was. "What was he saying to you?"

Juliana tried to hide a giggle behind her hand. "He's not arranged to marry me if that's what you're thinking."

Ana frowned. *Why would she think that?* She thought. "No," she replied with the frown still on her face. "I just did not understand a word he said to you."

Juliana stopped laughing instantly and looked at Ana in wide-eyed shock. *But she...* she thought. She shook her head to dispel the thought. "He was just reminding me of other duties I have to attend to." She guided Ana around the next corner and into the bathing rooms. She pointed out where the soaps were and where she could find the towel and clothes that were put out for her were waiting. "No one is due to bathe until the sun goes down, so take your time."

"Aren't you going to bathe?" She really didn't want to be alone, mainly because she would not be able to understand anyone who came in.

Juliana shook her head. "No, sorry," she apologized. "I must get onto the duties the prince reminded me of." She went to the door and opened it slightly. "If I'm not back by the time you're done, feel free to ask anyone to guide you back to your room if you need."

Ana could understand her reasoning. "Thank you."

With one more look at Ana, Juliana slipped out of the room.

"Something isn't right about this," she muttered to herself before going to do what the prince had asked of her.

Chapter 3

"What do you think of the girl I decided to take in?"

Ramses turned to look at the man everyone said he looked like when he was his age. And Ramses could believe it. The only obvious differences were the greying hair, the wisdom in his eyes, and the laughter lines around his father's eyes. "What are you planning, Father?" he asked, seeing the sparkle in his father's eyes.

"I'm not planning anything," Menes said, looking at his son in disbelief. "What makes you ask?"

Ramses looked at him incredulously. "The last time you had that look in your eyes, you had taken me to the Nile without the guards, and I had almost drowned."

Menes sighed. "I'm truly not planning anything." He walked down from the throne he was sitting in and grabbed Ramses by the shoulders. "I just wish to know what my son thinks about the girl I have taken into my protection."

Ramses himself sighed. "If I had not seen the girl for myself, I would have told you that you were a fool as you don't know if this girl would be a threat or not." He hesitated.

"But?" Menes prompted seeing reluctance in his son's eyes and hearing it in his voice.

"But I saw her when I told Juliana you wanted to see her as soon as possible." He thought back on the other girl he had seen. He remembered the way she had looked at him when he spoke. A frown appeared on his face as he remembered. *Was that really confusion I saw?* he thought to himself.

"Are you okay, Son?"

His father's question pulled him from his thoughts. Blinking, he looked up to his father. "I'm fine," he responded slowly. "Just thinking about something, that is all. Why do you ask?"

"You don't normally frown unless something is bothering you."

"Just unsure if I saw something correctly."

Menes didn't say another word on the subject. He knew that Ramses would talk when he was ready to. He then started to glance at the doors every so often. "Speaking of Juliana. Where is she?"

Again, a question from his father pulled Ramses from his thoughts. "Last I saw her; she was still taking the girl to the bathing rooms."

Before Menes could say anything, the doors to the throne room were opened quickly, and Juliana came running in. "I'm sorry, my Pharaoh," she apologized, dropping a small bow before coming to a stop beside Ramses. "Sorry I took so long."

"Just breathe, Juliana," Menes said softly. "You have nothing to apologize for. The girl was your first priority."

Juliana nodded and attempted to slow her breathing. After a couple of minutes, she was able to speak without her words coming out in gasps. "Her name is Ana." She paused.

She knew that Menes would not bring harm to Ana, but she wondered if it would be a good idea to tell of her worries.

"Whatever it is you're thinking, you can tell us," Ramses reassured the girl he saw as a sister. "We will not have all the information needed if we don't hear everything."

Juliana nodded, still unsure if it was a good thing to tell of her worries. "As I said, her name is Ana. She came here because she had some family issues back home, most likely in Rome, that she had to get away from." She paused to gather her thoughts. "But I believe that is only part of the story. I do know, from tears in her eyes, that something tragic happened."

Menes and Ramses both stood in silence as they reflected on what they were told.

"How do you figure she's from Rome?" Menes eventually asked.

"I spoke to her in Roman, and she asked how I could speak her language even though I lived here."

"What made you speak Roman?"

Juliana opened her mouth to answer but had to pause. What had made her speak Roman? Thinking about it, she really had no answer for it. "I honestly don't know," she answered. "It came to me naturally. Now that I think back, I thought I was speaking Egyptian until she pointed it out."

"What happened when I spoke near the bathing rooms?" Ramses asked, finally getting his head around the information given to him.

"What are you talking about?" Menes asked, instantly worried about the girl he had taken in. He turned to Juliana and gave her a stare that meant 'tell me or I'll put you on floor duty'. "What happened near the bathing rooms?"

"Apart from Ramses telling me to come and see you as soon as possible, nothing." Juliana paused. "Except for learning that Ana does not understand Egyptian."

Silence fell over the throne room.

"I'm sorry," Menes stuttered in a way that was seen as inappropriate for a Pharaoh. "Could you repeat that? I thought I heard you say – " He could not comprehend what he was just told. *But that doesn't make sense*, he thought.

"That she is unable to understand what we say," Ramses finished what his father had started to say. He thought it explained some things, like the confusion on Ana's face. But he also did not understand how she could not know the Egyptian language.

"It's true," Juliana confirmed. "She said, 'I just did not understand a word he said to you'."

Ramses sighed. "It explains why she looked confused when I spoke to you," he told Juliana.

"Also why I had to show her what I said earlier," Menes continued.

Juliana nodded to both men, and the room fell silent again.

"But," Ramses broke the silence. Menes and Juliana looked at him. "I don't see how that's possible."

"I agree with you," Menes said. "What have you seen?"

"Her dress. Even though it looks like rags, something about it just screams high rank. Her looks are too fair to be anything less than a noble."

"The way she walks and holds herself," Menes recalled. "It reminds me of how I would walk when my father was alive. She had the air of confidence around her. Usually, no one below nobility could walk like that."

"And this all means?" Juliana asked. She already knew what they meant. She wanted them to say it out loud. To Juliana, it was obvious as soon as she had seen Ana looking at the murals of the gods that she was of nobility or royalty.

"That she's of noble birth," Ramses whispered.

"Or royal birth," Menes continued. "But how could we have missed seeing that then?"

"It could be that the main class of society you associate with on a daily basis is the 'common' class," Juliana suggested. "You might have gotten used to their behaviour so that when faced with something different, you put it to the back of your mind."

"Possible," Menes conceded with Ramses nodding in agreement.

"What are we going to do now?" Ramses asked.

"We help her acclimatize. Teach her our language and customs." He paused to think. *Who would be better?* He thought. "Juliana. I want you to go with the girl everywhere. In a way, be a personal servant but also her friend. I also want you to teach her all she needs to know."

"Of course, my Pharaoh," Juliana said with a slight bow. "Shall I go and start my duties now?"

"Yes. I think that will be a good idea." Again, Juliana gave a bow. "I wonder what happened to her," he said as Juliana left the room.

"I would advise you not to meddle in affairs that do not require your meddling," Ramses advised his father.

Menes seemed to ignore what his son had said. Ramses sighed and, knowing he wouldn't be able to get through to his father, left the throne room.

"I need to meddle in this affair, my son," he said as the doors closed behind Ramses. "I cannot allow any harm to come to the girl who has already wormed her way into our hearts."

Chapter 4

Red sheets. Red tiles. Red clothes. Everything around her was red. She couldn't get away from it.

The sight before her was not something she would wish for anyone to see. Wondering how anyone could be so cruel stumped her.

"Why?" she screamed, closing her eyes. "Why this?"

Two hands, one on each shoulder, grabbed her and shook.

Her eyes flashed open, and she attempted to dash forward to escape while screaming. She did not get far though, as she splashed face-first into the water surrounding her.

Wait, she thought, *water?* Lifting her head out of the water and looking around the room, she started to calm down. Large stone bricks with carvings. Pillars with hawk-headed people. She wasn't in Rome anymore. She was in Egypt. Most importantly, she was safe.

"Ana?" a soft voice asked from behind her. She spun around in panic. "Are you okay?"

Juliana's soft voice penetrated through the panic. "I'm sorry," she sighed, focusing on the girl in front of her. "Just a very bad dream. I'm fine now."

"Do you want to talk about it?"

Ana rapidly shook her head. She believed that the sooner she got the dream out of her head, the better.

"Okay," Juliana said soothingly. "Let's get you dressed and back to your room."

Ana drew a deep breath. "Yes, please."

Juliana helped her out of the water and passed her a towel.

"May I ask who that belongs to?" Ana asked, spying the dress Juliana was holding out for her. It, like the clothes the Prince and the Pharaoh wore, was high quality. It was jewelled intricately, yet delicately done.

"I believe it once belonged to the late Queen," Juliana answered with a thoughtful look on her face.

Ana's eyes widened in shock and horror. "No," she stuttered. "I mean, I couldn't possibly – I wouldn't want to dis –" She knew the way she was speaking was not fit for someone of her status.

"We must always speak in full sentences, my daughter," her father would say when he caught her stuttering. "It is proper for a lady of your standing to finish what you wish to say."

Tears filled her eyes and spilled over her cheeks, thinking of her father. How she missed him.

"Ana?" Juliana asked.

"I'm okay," she replied thickly. "I was just thinking about my father." She cleared her throat and wiped the tears away with the towel. "About the dress. I couldn't possibly wear it. I don't want to dishonour the late Queen by wearing her clothes."

"The Pharaoh insisted you be given clothes better than what you arrived in. He gave me this dress for you to wear."

Ana sighed. *Do they really think I'm good enough to wear such high-quality clothing?* She asked herself. "If he insisted, then I really have no choice."

Juliana helped Ana to dress. She knew that even though the garments of Rome and Egypt were similar, there were slight differences that would make dressing difficult.

"I know you have been here less than one day," Juliana started when the two girls were almost back in the room Ana was given. "But how are you finding it here so far?"

Ana thought carefully about how to answer. "It's different," she said eventually. "I had heard that it was harsh living here in Egypt. It wasn't because of a lack of resources. There's plenty from what I've seen. No, it was the ruler, the Pharaoh, that made it hard." The two entered the room when they reached the door, and Ana sighed, sitting on the bed. "But it's nothing like that. The people in the village are flourishing, and the Pharaoh is kind, understanding, and generous. This is nothing like the stories I heard growing up."

"What you heard was true," Juliana stated.

Ana looked at her in shock and disbelief. Had she read everything wrong? Was this really the place she wanted to be?

"To an extent," Juliana hurriedly assured her, seeing her expression. "The previous Pharaoh repeatedly raised the taxes on the people. He demanded that half of every crop was to be kept by those living in the palace." She sat down next to Ana. "The people eventually revolted against him.

When the current Pharaoh, Menes, took the throne, he nursed the nation back to the prosperity it once had."

Before either Ana or Juliana could say anything else, the Pharaoh, who Ana now knew as Menes, swept into the room. He was talking at a rapid rate. Ana believed that even if she knew the language, she would not have been able to understand what was said because of the speed with which he spoke.

In her confusion, she did not notice when Prince Ramses walked in behind his father. She did notice him, however, when he spoke to his father.

Menes stopped speaking and looked at Ana. Seeing for himself her confused look, he gave her a sheepish one.

Did Ramses admonish his own father? She wondered. She would have surely been put over her father's knee if she had done that.

Blinking, she turned to Juliana. "Did you catch anything he said?" she asked slowly. "He spoke a bit too fast for me to understand."

Juliana giggled, which caused Menes to glare at the two girls playfully. "In short," she said, "he said that he was glad that the two of us were here." She then turned to Menes and Ramses and said something to them. Menes replied in turn. Nodding, Juliana looked back at Ana. "It has been recommended that I be your," she paused, "personal servant of sorts."

"No," Ana quickly disagreed, shaking her head. "I personally couldn't allow it."

"Maybe personal servant wasn't the correct term to use." Juliana sighed. "I will be your personal guide and tutor."

"How will that work?" Ana asked sceptically.

"I would go everywhere with you and show you around like a guide would. I would also teach you about the language and customs of Egypt."

Ana thought about what all that would mean for her. She'd have someone to show her the way around the palace. Someone would be helping her to fit in better. All in all, it seemed like a very good idea. "I agree," she said, causing Juliana to smile. "On one condition."

"Of course," Juliana nodded. If that was the only way for Ana to agree, Juliana would do anything.

"I refuse to allow you to attend to any duties that would be classified as jobs for a personal servant." She paused. "Agreed?"

"Agreed. I'll just let the Pharaoh know." She turned and, as much as Ana could guess, repeated the conversation they just had to Menes and Ramses.

Menes nodded with a thoughtful look. Suddenly, and quite without warning, his face gained a wide grin. He excitedly said something.

The one and only word she understood, was a name. From the name, she knew that it had something to do with Ramses. Looking at the said prince, she saw him nodding his head. Then he stopped nodding, his eyes widened, and he jerked to look at his father before exclaiming in surprise.

"What?" Ana prompted Juliana. "What did he say?"

"He said 'what'," Juliana answered.

"No, no, no." Ana shook her head. "Not him. What did Menes say?"

Hearing his name, Menes stopped smirking and looked curiously to Ana. Ramses followed his father's example, stopped glaring, and turned to Ana.

"He said that Ramses would help with your lessons when I'm not available, especially with the customs."

Ana's head, as if on its own accord, turned toward Ramses. Her wide eyes met his equally wide eyes.

Chapter 5

Lessons came and went as months flew by.

Ana could not believe how fast the time she had spent in Egypt had gone. She even enjoyed her lessons, which was something she never did back home.

Back home, it was always 'women do this; women do that'. Here it was 'this usually happens', 'on these special occasions that changes'.

Because of a newfound liking for learning new things, she found herself remembering her lessons easier and being eager for the next one.

Both Juliana and Ramses had commented on how well she had retained her new knowledge. According to the two, she had caught onto the language fairly early in her time in the palace. She had remembered most of the vocabulary and was very fluent in speaking. Someone who did not know that Ana was not from Egypt would have believed that she was born there.

She had managed to learn which hieroglyphs corresponded with which letter or which number. However, she was still trying to learn and remember the hieroglyphs for letter combinations.

"You're doing better than my parents did when they moved here," Juliana had said one lesson when Ana had gotten frustrated. "Father said it took them a year to learn the alphabet alone."

Although Juliana was an excellent tutor when it came to the verbal and written Egyptian language, it was discovered very early on in the lessons that she did not have the knack for teaching Ana the customs of the Egyptian people.

Thankfully Ramses was more than happy to step into Juliana's place and teach Ana himself.

Ana found herself understanding the customs lessons more when Ramses taught her than Juliana. Where Juliana would try and link and relate everything she was talking about back to similar or related Roman customs, Ramses would tell it like it is through stories. She would laugh at the misfortunes of some and ask questions in others. This would then generally lead to him telling her another story to help her understand.

"I have nothing else to teach you," Ramses said at the conclusion of a lesson just over two months into her stay. "You have mastered everything I had to tell you."

That did not stop their nightly storytelling though. Neither understood the reason behind it, but they found themselves unable to stay away from each other.

Over the course of the months, she had gotten quite close with everyone within the palace. The staff and the residents all loved her and would go out of their way to assist her with any needs she had. Even Pharaoh Menes would take time out of his busy schedule to spend with her.

Though no one knew exactly who she was.

Ana knew there would come a day when she would have to tell everyone she was lying to them. Yes, there were some things she had said that were true. But lies of omission are still lies.

She knew that the guards who had followed her to Egypt would have made it back to Rome and told him where she was. Then the time would come when the truth would come out. And she hoped that time would come later rather than sooner. Unfortunately for Ana, her hopes were shattered on the eve of her fifth month in Egypt.

"Important message for you, my Pharaoh," a guard from the palace gate informed Menes during the evening meal.

"Thank you," Menes thanked the guard and took the message.

The guard bowed with his left foot forward and left the room.

Looking at the scroll, Menes made a sound of surprise.

"What is it, Father?" Ramses asked. "Who is it from?"

"It's the official seal of Rome," Menes replied. Ana tensed at hearing this. "We haven't had any dealings with Rome that have needed the official seal for a while."

Juliana noticed the tense Ana beside her and discretely took her hand in comfort.

Breaking the seal, Menes unrolled the scroll. Deciding not to have to repeat himself, he read the scroll out loud.

Pharaoh,

It has come to my notice that a traitor to the Roman Empire has been seen within the boundaries of your kingdom.

They have been charged with high treason for the murder of our previous Emperor.

We, the people of the Roman Empire, would appreciate it if you could apprehend the traitor for us and hold them until I personally can bring her back to Rome for her trial.

Your Ally,
Claudius
Emperor of Rome

Silence echoed through the throne room, each occupant with different thoughts running through their minds.

Menes and Ramses were wondering how anyone could kill Emperor Antonius and why they were not informed of his passing.

Ana was shaking in fear and rage, thinking of ways she would be able to commit the crime she had been accused of and not be found out.

Juliana saw Ana shaking. She knew there was a chance that Ana was a high ranking of some level. But could there be a chance that she was somehow related to the royal family themselves?

Ana, still shaking from head to toe, couldn't stand to sit in silence any longer than she already had been. She abruptly stood up, the force of it causing the chair she had been sitting on to crash to the floor.

The other three in the room jumped at the sudden noise and the seemingly nonsense she was saying.

Having heard the crash, the guards stationed outside the door rushed inside, ready to fight off an intruder. They froze, however, when they spotted Ana moving around the room in what they would describe as a rant.

"All is fine," Menes assured the guards in a dismissive tone.

They bowed to their Pharaoh and slowly backed out of the room, keeping an eye on Ana.

"What is she saying?" Ramses asked Juliana once the guards had left and the door was closed.

The girl in question was pacing and speaking in Roman nervously.

"Mostly, it's not making any sense to me," Juliana replied. "But I did make out her saying 'don't let them come' and 'don't let them take me'." Suddenly Ana took on an aggressive tone and threw her arms around in a fit of rage. Juliana, Menes, and Ramses could only stare in astonishment. No one had seen her as angry as she was in any of her time in the palace. "I'm not the traitor," Juliana quickly translated. "You're the traitor. You're the one who did the killing."

In an impulsive move, Ramses got up from his seat and gently grabbed Ana from behind to stop her pacing and try and help her to calm down.

Feeling the comforting arms around her, although not realizing who it was holding her, she started to calm down. Soon she was relaxed enough and sank into the embrace of Ramses standing behind her.

None in the room noticed the smug look and mischievous smirk on the Pharaoh's face.

Chapter 6

"I'm sorry," Ana apologized in Egyptian once she had completely calmed down. "I did not mean to lose my temper the way I did."

"We understand," Ramses said, still standing behind and holding her. She made no action to move out of his embrace, which pleased Ramses in ways he had never felt before. "From what we could gather from what Juliana was able to translate, the anger was completely called for."

Ana looked at Juliana, horrified. "What did you translate?" she asked.

"How about you tell us the story behind your outburst," Menes offered gently. "Then we'll tell you what we know."

Ana took a deep breath and unconsciously put her hands over Ramses's to gather strength.

"I may not have been entirely truthful to you when I first arrived." She paused. A squeeze of her hands from Ramses gave her the courage to continue. "My full name is Liviana, but those close to me would call me Ana. I am the eldest child and only daughter of Emperor Antonius. Claudius, the one who sent the scroll, is my younger brother."

"Growing up, the two of us were always close. We would attend our lessons together and be there for each

37

other when it was needed. No matter what happened, we were inseparable."

"But then everything changed. When I was twelve, and he was ten, he suddenly drifted away. And it wasn't just from me. It was from Father as well. The only time he would associate with us was at meal times. Even then, it was with reluctance on his part. Father nor I knew what was wrong with him."

"It took us a couple of years to find out. The two of us were shocked to say the least. How could someone, so adverse to having an army, do that?"

She didn't know how to continue. Even a year on, she still could not understand her brother's actions.

Menes, Ramses, and Juliana could not wrap their heads around what they had heard. They knew that Ana had to have been high ranking in society. But to have been housing a potential heir to the Roman throne was not what they were expecting.

Ana cleared her throat to give herself more confidence, and everyone's head snapped to face her again. "There he was, standing amongst the soldier with a sword held expertly in his hands," she continued. "It was as if he had been training his whole life. As I said, Father and I could not believe what we were seeing."

"When we asked him about it that night at dinner, all he said was that he was getting bored with normal lessons. He needed something new to learn. Then he stormed out of the dining hall."

"And with that, all communications with Claudius ceased. For a year, we didn't see hide nor hair of my brother. We knew he was still in Rome though. How couldn't we, with all the soldiers making comments about the youngest boy in the army reaching the rank of General. He had just turned fourteen."

"It was approximately four months before my arrival here that the real problem started." She took a deep breath, and comfort from the arms still around her, to be able to continue. "I was waiting in the dining hall for Father one night for dinner. It was starting to get late, and Father still had not arrived. This wasn't unusual. As Emperor, he had a lot of work to do, lose track of time and have dinner in his study. But he would usually send a servant to let me know."

"I was starting to get worried. I made my way to his study, as that was the last place I had seen him. Coming up to his door, all I could hear was silence. My first thought was that he had fallen asleep. He'd done it before."

"I slowly opened the door, still thinking he was asleep. But all I saw was red." She couldn't hold the tears back.

The others did not have to think hard about what she meant by the last sentence.

No child, no matter how old they are, should ever have to find their parents like that, Menes thought, watching the crying girl who had fallen to the ground in his son's arms.

It took the combined effort of Ramses and Juliana for Ana to stop crying.

"I'm sorry," she apologized. "I should not have lost it so much."

Menes knelt down to Ana's height and gently took her hands into his. "There is no need to apologize," he soothed. "What you saw is something no child should have to find."

"You don't have to continue if you don't feel as if you can," Juliana said from her left.

Ana fiercely shook her head. "No. I'm Liviana, Princess of Rome. If I can't get through this, then I won't be able to handle facing my brother when he arrives."

"You mentioned that he was the traitor," Ramses said, knowing that Ana wouldn't be able to handle more talk about how she found her father. "What did you mean by that?"

"Exactly that. When he came and found me later, he confessed that he had killed our father."

"Apparently, he had heard that the people did not feel as if his rule was helping Rome to be prosperous. Personally, I believe this to be Claudius's own views, not that of the people. He said that his own policies and rulings would be better for the empire. And what better way, he said, than to kill the current emperor and take the throne for himself."

"But he did not know that Father had done something unorthodox." The others looked at her in shock. She nodded. "He had decreed that should he die; I would take the throne in his place."

"Naturally, when he found this out, Claudius was furious. He knew there had to be a way for him to sit on the throne. But, as I had not decreed who would succeed me, he could not kill me as he had Father."

"So, he went for 'the next best thing'. He proposed that I marry him." The eyes of Juliana, Menes and Ramses bugged out of their heads. "I refused." The three of them sighed in relief. "After months of him nagging me about marriage, I ran away."

"I knew he would have guards follow me. So, I did the only thing I could think of to lose them. I went to the port and boarded a ship that was bound for anywhere outside the empire."

"I did not know they were on the same ship until I reached your port. When I saw them, I ran." She looked down at her feet, refusing to look at any of the others in the room. "And here we are a couple of months later."

"That's quite the tale," Menes said after a long pause.

Liviana closed her eyes in fear. She knew what was going to happen. She knew that her next few breaths would be the last free air she would breathe.

Gentle hands were placed on her shoulders. "But we believe you."

Menes's gentle, reassuring tones pulled her from her fear. "But how can you believe me?" Liviana asked. "I could have made the whole thing up."

"No sane person would be able to spin a story like yours," Ramses said from where he was still kneeling behind her. "Especially with as much emotion and detail as you put into it."

"But how does that help me? Claudius isn't going to stop until he has me by his side and he's sitting on the throne of Rome."

"There is one way," Menes said hesitantly. "There's an old law that states a Pharaoh is allowed to pardon someone of past accusations."

Ramses sighed. "One problem with your plan Father," he stated. "The one being pardoned has to be married to a fairly high-class Egyptian."

"Again, I ask how this can help me," Liviana said, close to tears for another time that day. "Who of high standing would want to marry someone who left everything behind and ran from her home?"

At Liviana's question, Menes openly smirked at her and Ramses. The two of them knew that nothing good could come from that smirk. "Why Ramses will, of course."

Chapter 7

For the month after Menes declared that Liviana would marry Ramses, time passed slowly for the pair of young Royals.

Over the month, the two of them had gotten closer to each other. It was inevitable, they agreed. Especially when they had been left alone to plan their wedding.

"I can't take it anymore," Ramses groaned one day while storming into the room in which Liviana was sitting.

Ana blinked a couple of times while watching Ramses pace in front of her. The words rang in her head. *I can't take it anymore*. Slowly, she stood up and grabbed his hands to stop him from pacing. Fear over how he would answer her question almost stopped her from asking. "What can't you take anymore?" she asked, fighting through her fear.

"This," Ramses answered, letting go of one of Ana's hands and waving it between them.

Ana let her old self break through. She dropped the other hand, stormed to where Ramses had put his crown, picked it up, and thrust it into his chest. "If that is how you truly feel," she seethed and pointed to the door, "take all that you brought with you and show yourself out the door. I will go to your father and tell him the agreement was nullified for personal reasons and find somewhere else that may be able to help me." Ramses opened his mouth to say something. Ana though, did not allow him to utter his first word. "No," she demanded. "I have heard stories of men who tried to talk their ways out of a tight spot only for the women to get hurt when he does not keep his promises."

"That is not what I meant," he implored. This time Ramses cut off Ana as she went to say something. She gave an indignant sound as a hand covered her mouth. "I did not mean 'this' as in anything between the two of us." He swallowed hard. He had no understanding of how other men made confessing look easy. "I meant that I could not stand the closeness we have, yet I'm unsure of where we stand with each other."

Ramses dropped his hand and paused to allow Ana to say something in return.

Ana blinked a couple of times, trying to process what she was told. "What are you talking about?" she asked, confused. "We're as close as we are because we get along well. What else is there to it?"

Ramses let out a small groan. "I don't know how to properly say what I'm trying to."

"There's one thing you need to know about me," Ana said, staring at Ramses in a way he could not interpret. "I prefer it when people tell me exactly what's on their minds instead of skirting the edges and confusing everyone in the process."

Ramses took a deep breath. "I love how close we have become," he said. "But I have found myself wanting for us to be closer than we already are."

"How close do you mean?" Ana whispered.

"With how similar our thoughts and ideas have been this past month; I would not mind if you were my only wife. I would prefer it, in fact."

"But-" Ana was confused. "But I heard that the Kings of Egypt had more than one wife. The main one to sit beside him in meetings, yes, but others should he need to produce an heir."

"That is usually the case, yes," Ramses confessed, impressed by how much Ana had learnt about the Egyptian culture. "It has been known in the past for a King to have only one wife. Personally, I don't care if I do not have an heir. All I care about is living my life how I want it with the woman I want to live it with."

Ana smiled and held Ramses's hand in hers. "For someone who had no idea how to say something, you did a perfectly good job of it." A thought came to her, and she frowned. "How will everyone react to this? What will they say? What will they think? Will they even allow this to happen?"

"Ana," Ramses gently stopped her. "Why does it matter what people think or say? How does it affect us how people react, or whether they allow this to happen or not?"

"The people, the council, and the families always judge every little thing that an individual does. No one is safe from the ever-watchful eyes of everyone else. If a partnership is not approved of, it does not happen."

"That may have been how it was back in Rome. But it does not matter here in Egypt. No matter how much I try to avoid it, the people view us as the living embodiment of Horus, a God living amongst them. And really, who can question the will of a god?"

"Taking that role a little too literally, aren't you?" She sighed. "Your father is the one who has the final say though. What if he doesn't agree to this plan of yours?"

"He takes my thoughts and feelings into consideration when making choices for me."

"I don't want to say anything though." Ana put her head down with her eyes cast at the floor. "Just in case of the event that he does not approve."

"Then we won't." Ramses pulled Ana into a hug. She rested her head on his chest. "Then we won't."

Unbeknown to the two royals in the chamber, one sneaky servant had heard the whole conversation and confessions and had run off to tell the Pharaoh.

Chapter 8

Later that day, Liviana and Ramses were sitting at the table in the room going over the final arrangements for the wedding, when a guard knocked on the door.

"The Pharaoh has requested the presence of the two of you in the throne room," the guard informed them.

Looking at each other, Ana and Ramses stood up and began the walk to the throne room, thanking the guard as they passed him.

"What do you think he wishes to speak to us about?" Ana asked halfway to their destination.

"I don't have any ideas," Ramses answered. "When I spoke to him at the end of breakfast this morning, he said that there was nothing to worry about and that everything was going according to plan. Whatever that meant really. The only plan of his that I know about is the two of us getting married."

"And he left everything up to us," Ana interrupted. "And he only told us to let him know when everything was planned."

"Exactly." Ramses sighed. "Sometimes, I have no clue as to what goes on in my father's mind. Not that I want to at times."

The pair continued their walk in silence, with Ana staring in wonder. Even after living in the Palace for months, she still could not get over how intricate and detailed the walls were. Where Romans put a lot of effort into their mosaic floors, the Egyptians put extreme effort into their paintings and statues.

At the ornately carved, gold-plated doors of the throne room, the two of them stopped. The guards standing watch were looking anxious, their eyes darting to the doors in worry.

"How is he?" Ramses asked the guards.

"He seems angry, my Prince," the guard on the left side of the door answered.

"We've been hearing muttering and sighing since he asked for your presence," the guard on the right continued.

Ana and Ramses themselves cast worried looks at each other.

Ramses sighed and turned back to the doors and guards. "Let my father know we're here," he softly commanded.

The guards put their left foot forward and placed their right hand over their hearts. With a bow of their heads, they opened the doors and stood in front of them. "Prince Ramses and Princess Liviana as requested, my Pharaoh," the left guard announced.

"Send them in," came a grumpy reply from within.

"Good luck," the right guard whispered as the two royals passed through the doors.

Ana gave a small smile in thanks as the guards closed the door behind them.

Within the room, the Pharaoh was pacing in front of his throne. Now that they were in the room with Menes, Ana and Ramses could hear what the guards were talking about.

While pacing, Menes was muttering under his breath, and with every third or fourth pass of the throne, he let out a heavy sigh.

"Father," Ramses attempted to get Menes's attention. Menes gave another great sigh and continued pacing. Ramses looked to Ana for help, but she shrugged, not knowing what to do to help. He decided to try to get his father's attention again. "Father." This time Menes stopped pacing and turned to glare at his son. "What seems to be the problem, Father?"

Menes started to pace again. This time though, it seemed he had a purpose and was putting more effort behind each step. "You would not *believe* what I have heard," he stressed, emphasizing the believe.

"What have you h – "

Menes cut Ramses off. "How dare this happen within my own home. And right under my nose no less." He turned his back to the younger royals and clasped his hands behind his back. "I cannot believe this is happening. Everything is all going," he turned around, shocking Ramses and Ana with a large smile, "according to my plan."

Ramses and Ana were too shocked to say anything for a while. Ana was the one to break the silence with the question plaguing both their minds. "What plan are you talking about? If you don't mind me asking, sir."

"The plan that got you here, of course."

"What are you saying, Father?" Ramses questioned. He thought back over all of his father's plans, and none of them involved him and Ana standing in front of him, confused out of their minds. "You haven't spoken to me of any such plans."

"Of course, I have." At the blank stares he was receiving, Menes sighed. "Remember a month ago when I proposed that the two of you get married?" They nodded. "What I saw that day was what made me think of the marriage plan. Ana, I don't know if you realized it, but whenever you had physical contact with Ramses, you seemed to either calm down or gain the courage to explain something. And you Ramses, my boy. You gravitated toward her like a moth to a flame. You were there when she needed to be calmed or when she needed encouragement." The younger royals looked at each other, bewildered. "I have only ever seen one other couple act like that when they first met."

"You and Mother," Ramses interrupted. This time it was Menes's turn to look shocked. "The guards and servants would always tell me stories of the two of you whenever I asked." Menes smiled wistfully.

"I hope you don't mind me asking," Ana started. "But what happened to the Queen?"

"She died in childbirth." He paused to take a deep breath. "And I was that child."

"It was not your fault," Menes implored. "Your mother was very ill for the majority of her pregnancy. She had contracted a disease from one of the servants. And her health had never been the best since she was a child." All of them paused in solemn silence. "But enough about the past. How are the two of you coming along with the wedding planning?"

"We had everything planned and finalized moments before you summoned us," Ramses responded with a smile.

"Not everything," Ana contradicted. "We still haven't organized the feast nor the dress I will be wearing."

Menes chuckled. "Have the two of you looked out over the village lately?" Both Ramses and Ana shook their heads. "The people have been bustling about preparing meals in the hopes they will be the ones chosen to make the ceremonial feast."

"Have any been presented to the palace cooks Father?" Ramses asked after a quick look shared with Ana.

"Not that I have been made aware of, no. Why?"

"Let's not disappoint anyone then, as well as saving the cook the trouble of tasting hundreds of dishes, and allow all villagers who wish to prepare food, to do so," Ana replied with a smile.

"That's a brilliant idea," Menes beamed. "How do you feel about giving the village the chance to witness a Royal Wedding?"

"Fine with me," Ramses agreed, with Ana nodding beside him.

"Perfect. Now about your dress. I can have a dress ready for you by the time of the wedding in two days."

"But sire-"

Menes interrupted her with a raised hand. "I keep telling you to call me Father. And it's no problem with the dress." Menes smiled sweetly, causing Ana to smile back. "Now, as it is tradition for the bride and groom to not see each other the day before the wedding, I suggest the two of you go and spend as much time together as you can today."

Ramses and Ana nodded in thanks before heading for the door. "Wait!" Ana exclaimed when Ramses opened the door. "I wanted to ask about – "

"No need to worry about it," he answered, interrupting her again. "You wouldn't be the first Great and Only Wife that a Pharaoh has had."

Chapter 9

Two days later, Liviana was anxiously pacing in her room, waiting for the Pharaoh to come in, take her to the throne room, and get the wedding started.

She knew that the events of today were going to be spoiled by some unwanted guests. The day before, the guards had come running to the Pharaoh to inform him that there was a troop of Roman soldiers traversing across the land on foot, and would be at the city on the evening of the wedding. Therefore, Ana was going to make the most of the good times as she could before everything went sour, as her father would say before he died.

The only problem was that, although she was anxiously waiting, there was still no dress for her to wear. Menes had said that he would have a dress for her in time. Although she believed that he would be able to get a dress for her, Ana had her doubts that he would actually be able to.

The sun was starting to peek over the edges of the land, and it was planned for her to be at the doors of the throne room by the time the sun had completely risen over the horizon. It didn't look like she wasn't going to get to her own wedding on time.

Her pacing was interrupted by the door to her room opening. She spun around to face the person who dared to enter without knocking, only to sigh in relief as Menes came through the door with material hanging over one of his arms.

"I'm sorry about bringing this to you so late," he apologized, holding the material, which turned out to be a dress, up. "The servants I gave it to took extra care to wash it multiple times to make sure that it was fit for you to wear. I didn't receive it until just before Ra started to rise."

"It's beautiful," Ana breathed. The top of the dress was a fine silky material with golden beads sewn into it in an intricate but delicate pattern of swirls. The bottom of the dress, from the knees down, was thin and see-through. "Where did you get it?" She took the dress from his hands and went behind the changing divider to change into it.

"Don't worry about that," he replied. "All that you need to worry about is getting through the day and being happy in your freedom."

"I will get the answer out of you at some point today." She came out from behind the screen, the dress fitting perfectly and her golden hair flowing over her shoulders.

"And you will. Just not right at this very minute."

Juliana came running into the room like a storm. "I am so sorry," she rushed. "I thought I would collect your dress from the wash only to be told that it had already been taken. I have been running around the palace trying to locate it. I was starting to worry it had been lost. Then by some miracle, one of the other servants told me they had seen the Pharaoh carrying the dress to your room. But I was on – "

"Juliana," Ana interrupted. "It's fine. I believe all that occurred because you were not properly informed about who was getting the dress for me."

"I thought it would be logical that I, as your guide and closest friend, would get the dress and bring it to you."

Ana gave a mischievous smile before speaking to Juliana in Roman. "It seems a certain crown-wearing male in the room was of the same or similar opinion."

Juliana adopted a mischievous smile of her own and replied the same way. "Well, I guess it makes sense. It is the dress his wife wore at their wedding."

Ana's smile turned into a glare which she turned on Menes, who looked confused at the conversation the girls were having, then nervous at the glare he was getting. "He failed to mention that," she said, switching back to Egyptian.

"Well, whatever it is I didn't mention can surely wait until after the ceremony," Menes said with a nervous smile. "Ra has almost fully risen, and it is best not to be late or else anger the gods."

Chapter 10

If Liviana was honest with herself, she would have to say that the ceremony was all a blur to her. From the moment Menes mentioned the time, everything seemed to shift out of focus. She hadn't noticed Menes and Juliana had led her out of her room and toward the throne room. She didn't see the large golden doors open or the group of assembled nobles who had come to witness the royal wedding. She hadn't heard the long speech the High Priest made or the vows Ramses and herself were asked to repeat.

She was brought back into the present when the High Priest said, "May the goddess Bast and the goddess Hathor bless this marriage with many years of happiness and grant you the gift of having children."

Ramses, noticing that Ana was not in the right frame of mind from the beginning of the ceremony, placed a hand on her back and guided her toward the gathered nobles. The nobles then gave a massive cheer for the newly wedded prince and his bride.

Ana, now realizing what was going on, knew that the next step was to present themselves to the people, who had surely been crowding outside the palace since well before Ra had even begun to rise above the horizon.

"Are you okay?" Ramses quietly asked on their way to the balcony.

"I'm fine," Ana replied. "Why do you ask?"

Ramses smiled. "You just seemed to be going through the actions from the moment you stepped through the doors." He lost the smile and became nervous. "You're not having second thoughts, are you?"

"No." Ana hurriedly shook her head. "Nothing like that at all." She sighed. "It's just that, when your father mentioned that Ra had fully risen, the knowledge of my brother, or the guards under my brother's control, are going to be here in the near future numbed my brain."

Ramses gave a small chuckle, relieved that it wasn't anything as bad as he thought it was. "You don't have to worry about them. My father has his own plans for when they arrive. I have no idea what they are, but you can be rest assured that they are not going to take you away from here."

"Thank you," she sighed again and leant her head on his shoulder. "I think that's just what I needed to hear to be able to get through the rest of the day."

They stopped just inside the open doors to the balcony. Ramses wrapped his arms further around Ana and whispered in her ear. "Then only worry about how much talking you will have to do with the nobles after meeting the crowd."

"Then let's get that part over with quickly then," Ana replied with a smile.

Ramses nodded to the High Priest who had followed them from the altar.

He nodded back to the pair before walking onto the balcony and addressing the crowd. "People of Egypt. Today the gods have smiled upon us all. Today we have gathered for the bonding between our very own Prince Ramses and Princess Liviana of Rome." The crowd cheered wildly. They had awaited this day since the prince was of marrying age. The High Priest raised his hand, and the crowd quietened down. "May the gods bless them with long and happy lives. May they be blessed with many children. Blessed be the Gods."

"Blessed be the Gods," the crowd repeated as a whole.

"I ask our beloved Pharaoh Menes to come forth to say a few words."

Menes moved from his spot behind Ramses and Ana. The two of them hadn't even noticed that he was behind them the whole time. Menes let the people cheer for him for a couple of minutes before he raised a hand for silence. They fell silent almost instantly. "I have had the pleasure of watching these two people become closer over the last months. I have never seen two people more perfectly matched than the two of them." Ramses and Ana smiled at each other softly. "May the gods bless them with endless happiness and love. Blessed be by the gods."

"Blessed be the gods," the crowd replied again.

"Without any more interruptions, I now present to you His Royal Highness Prince Ramses and the Prince Consort Princess Liviana."

"Ready?" Ramses asked, removing his arm from around her and offering it to her.

"Ready," Ana replied, placing her hand on top of his hand.

Together they walked onto the balcony to face the crowd of people who had come to see the couple.

Upon the sight of them, the crowd exploded into loud cheering. This bout of cheering seemed louder than when the High Priest mentioned the marriage between the royals or even at the appearance of the Pharaoh.

Like his father, Ramses let the crowd cheer for a little bit before he raised his hand to them. Again, they fell silent almost instantly. "We thank you all for being here today. I know a lot of you have been here since Khonsu was high in the sky and before Ra had even thought about gracing us with his miraculous presence on this most special day of our people. We wish you all the same happiness that the gods have brought to Liviana and me over the last few months. May the gods bless all the celebrations that are about to occur in our honour. Blessed be." He finished with a bow toward the people.

To Ana's surprise, the entire crowd bowed back. Even after being in Egypt for many months, there were still things that shocked her. In Rome, a crowd of this many people would not even think to bow back to even the most loved Emperor, let alone his son.

When all of them were once again standing straight, Ramses looked toward his father, who nodded slightly in reply. He stepped forward again and addressed the people. "May the celebrations in your homes be grand and last well past the rise of Khonsu. As a thank you for your support and as a favour to Princess Liviana, the guards will soon open the gates, and you are all invited to join us in the grand hall for our celebrations."

The crowd, once again, began cheering. This time, there seemed to be many shouts of 'thank you' and 'blessed be'. Some of the children were even heard to have said, "Did you hear that? We get to go into the palace." The cheering went for a long period of time, well after all the royals and the High Priest had entered the palace again and rejoined the nobles.

Chapter 11

Menes knew that he had to avoid Liviana for as long as he could. He did not exactly know what it was that Juliana had told Ana, but he knew that he was in for a long talking to.

He mingled between the noble families and the other guests. When he saw that Ana was making her way to the group he was with, he would excuse himself and move on to the next group.

The cycle continued until Ra had set beneath the sand.

"You seem to be moving around the room a lot faster than you usually do," a voice from behind Menes said. He was so startled that he jumped and the crown on his head slipped off. He thought that his latest hiding spot was the best of the night: behind one of the tall pillars stretching from the floor to the ceiling, this one depicting a great victory of one of the Pharaoh's past.

Menes spun around to scold the person who dared sneak up on the Pharaoh. But the face was one that he had seen sneak up on himself and the others in the palace since the day he could walk.

"Could it be," the person continued, "that you are trying your hardest not to be cornered by a certain bride of the day?"

"I have no idea what you are talking about," Menes denied whilst looking around to make sure that Ana had not accompanied the person.

"Of course you don't, Father." Ramses had a large smirk on his face. "It just looked to me that you were scared to be seen in the same place as her."

"That's not the reason I don't want to be cornered."

If it was possible, the smirk on Ramses's face would have gotten larger. "So, you admit that you were moving around to avoid her." Menes's eyes got wider as Ramses continued speaking. He had realized what he had done. "Not a very nice thing to do, Father. Some might begin to think that you no longer accept Ana into the family."

Menes spun around again and glared at Ramses. "Very sneaky of you, my son." He placed his hand against his chin. "I wonder where you get that from," he pondered, not realizing he had spoken out loud.

"Yes," Ramses drawled. "I wonder too." He adopted the same pose as his father. "It couldn't have been the man who taught me to listen to the words spoken by others and then, if I need to, twist them to my advantage and make them tell me what I want to know." He looked at his father yet again. "Could it?"

Menes looked on, shocked and devastated. His mouth was hanging wide, and his hand was clasped over his heart. "Of all the things that I have taught you to become an excellent Pharaoh. Of all the things that you could have used against me. It had to have been that. It could not have been something else?"

"What could not have been something else?"

Both Menes and Ramses jumped at the voice that rang from behind. Their eyes widened in shock, and their hands flew to their hearts.

The voice then began to giggle. "You should have seen that reaction. I could not have planned it better."

"How could you do that?" Menes asked, spinning to glare at the offending person. "How dare you sneak up on the Pharaoh?"

"That's funny coming from said Pharaoh, who has been avoiding me all day and well into the night."

"I have not."

"Don't deny what you have already confessed to, Father," Ramses said, putting his arm around Ana's waist. "Why have you been moving around and not wanting to be caught with Ana?"

"It's not that I don't want to be caught." Menes really didn't want to talk about the reason that he had been moving around too fast to be socially acceptable.

"Could it be that you don't want me to speak to you about what Juliana told me this morning?" Ana asked teasingly.

"It could be. Except I have no idea about what she told you."

Ana turned to Ramses. "Did you know that your father let me wear a wedding dress that someone else wore to their wedding?"

Ramses' eyes widened before narrowing to glare at his father. "Did he now?"

"He did." Ana snuck a look at Menes. He looked on with wide eyes. "Not only that, did you know that it was worn by someone of great importance?"

Ramses's glare deepened. This wasn't a playful glare. He truly looked angry at his father. "How could you?" he seethed. "You had a whole month to have a dress made, and yet you do this?" He pulled in a calming breath. "Does this person even know what you have done?"

Menes sighed in defeat. "No." Ramses opened his mouth to say more. "Before you say anything," Menes interrupted. "I just wanted a piece of your mother to be here with us."

Ramses and Ana deflated at the confession. Menes truly looked miserable, with his eyes downcast and filling with tears.

Ana sighed. "You could have told me that from the start." She placed one of her hands on one of his shoulders. "If that was the reason behind the dress, I would not have argued. I wish my parents were here today too."

Menes lost the defeated look and smiled slightly. He looked to Ramses for reassurance. Ramses nodded his head with a smile of his own. The smile that Menes had, got bigger.

Before Menes could say anything, there was a loud commotion coming from further into the grand hall.

Chapter 12

"What is the meaning of this disturbance?" Menes bellowed when they reached the source of the commotion. Standing in the middle of the room was a man that was at least two years younger than Liviana.

The man turned to face Menes. "I demand that you hand over the traitor to me," he commanded.

Menes frowned in confusion. "I do not understand your meaning. What traitor?"

"I have it on very good authority that you have, within your palace, a highly dangerous criminal." He pointed his finger toward Menes's chest. "I demand that she be placed into the custody of my guards immediately."

"I still do not understand. I have not been housing any criminals to the best of my knowledge." Menes looked around the room and spotted Ramses standing close by with Ana. "What about you, Son? Have you seen any criminals?"

"Just the ones in our prisons, Father," Ramses replied. "But none from another nation."

The man turned and glared at Ramses. His expression changed to one of shock when he saw Ana in her dress. He turned back to Menes. "What is the meaning of this? Why is my traitor dressed as royalty?"

"Ana is dressed, as you say, as royalty because she is. She has been married to my son Ramses making her the new Prince Consort." The proud look Menes had adopted turned to one of suspicion. "What's it to you?"

"She," he yelled, pointing at Ana, "is the one I sent the message about. She is wanted for the crime of murder. She will be handed over to me to face trial back in Rome. If you do not heed my commands, there will be consequences." By this time, he was huffing from exertion.

"Oh yes," Menes drawled as if just remembering the message sent not one month previous. "It appears to now be null and void. By Egyptian Law, a Pharaoh is able to pardon anyone of any previous crimes they have committed by allowing them to marry one of their subjects, therefore making them one of their subjects." He gestured to Ana and Ramses. "As you can see, I have done so by them marrying each other."

If someone could have steam coming from their ears, this man would have it pouring out with how red his face was. "How absurd. That is the most ridiculous law I have ever heard." He reached out and pulled Ana to him. "It's not just murder she's being accused of. It's the murder of my father, Emperor Antonius."

"I think you have been mistaken, Claudius," Ana spoke for the first time. "Why would I kill my own father? I'm not the one who became hungry for power."

"You will only speak when spoken to." He shook her so hard that the jewels on the dress started to rattle.

"I have had enough of this," Ramses yelled. "Guards, remove this man from the Princess and escort him from the village."

The guards did as they were told. They gently pulled Ana away and violently shoved the man, now known as Claudius, from the room.

"I will get you, Liviana," Claudius screamed as he was pushed away. "You mark my words. You will be taken home."

"What happened in the past is in the past," Menes said calmly. "We must now look to the future. If you cannot accept that, then you are not welcome in my kingdom."

Claudius stomped his foot with a frustrated scream before storming from the room; the guards close behind.

Silence rang through the room for a few minutes longer.

"Let's not just stand here," Menes suggested. "Let the celebrations continue."

And they did, well past the rising of Khonsu until Ra was starting to rise.

Chapter 13

Silence from an enemy was always a troubling sign.

That was what Liviana's father used to tell her. It was always 'the calm before the storm'.

The first week of silence was normal for a leader who wanted to worry an enemy. That was the basics of Roman warfare when in another country. Show a front and wait some time before attacking.

The only problem for the royal family was that one week turned into one month very quickly.

"He's obviously planning something," the Royal Vizier announced when the first month had passed. "All he has done is make camp outside our city and do nothing."

Menes had a thoughtful look. He had seen this strategy used many times by the people while his father was Pharaoh. But they were people who did not have the military planning experience that a prince would have. "As much as I wish that to be true," he said. "I do not believe that to be the case for Prince Claudius." The vizier did not agree and opened his mouth to argue. "From what I have been told about the teachings in the Roman royal family, the prince would have been taught a wide range of strategies to intimidate his enemies." He turned to look at Ana standing beside Ramses. "Am I correct in my observations, my dear?"

"You are indeed, my Pharaoh," Liviana replied. "My father taught Claudius and I to always have more than one plan. Always have a backup plan for a backup plan, he said."

The vizier scoffed at the idea of the Pharaoh turning toward Liviana for advice. "Why would your father teach you the art of war? I have known many a family from Rome where the women were never allowed near men's discussions."

Ramses quickly stepped forward from his position beside his father. "How dare you speak to your princess in such a manner," he said.

Liviana gently placed a hand on his elbow. "It is alright, Husband," she soothed. "He does not understand that my father noticed that, from an early age, Claudius had no regard for the lives of those around him. He does not know that my father knew that Claudius would lead our nation to ruin should he be placed on the throne. Therefore, he does not know that my father, Emperor Antonius of Rome, had appointed me to be his successor and taught me everything an Empress should know to rule and defend my Empire." She turned to the vizier and said in a hard voice, "So, of course my father would teach me the art of war." The vizier paled. "Do you have any other problems with the Pharaoh turning to me for advice?"

The vizier quickly shook his head before rushing from the room when Menes dismissed him.

"That was very nicely handled, my dear," Menes complimented once the heavy door had closed. "Spoken like a true leader."

Liviana smiled. "It was something I picked up on while watching court sessions with my father. If one accused another of something without knowing all the facts, Father would calmly state said facts before essentially telling the accuser off with the obvious."

"What do you think he's doing then?" Ramses asked.

Liviana thought over the information and signs they had been given throughout the previous month. "I don't know exactly what he has planned. What he seems to be doing at the moment is waiting for something. What that something is, determines what plan he follows through with."

All three were silent as they contemplated what Claudius could be waiting for.

"It could be anything," Ramses sighed. "I can't think of anything he might be waiting for."

"It has to be something very specific," Menes said.

An idea hit Liviana like an arrow shot by a centurion. "You're right," she agreed. "He's waiting for something extremely specific." Neither man had caught the arrow yet. Liviana rolled her eyes. "What is it that he came here for?" Menes frowned in thought, but Ramses had a blank look on his face. Liviana sighed. "He came here to take me back to Rome."

Menes and Ramses's faces turned horrified.

"Then we must double the guard," Ramses demanded.

"No!" Liviana was very quick to dissuade.

"But, my dear," Menes started. "Now that we know you are his target, we must do all that we can to keep you safe."

Liviana shook her head. "I must refuse, my Pharaoh." Both men looked even more horrified. Liviana smiled gently. "If we increase my guard, Claudius will undoubtedly know that we have discovered his intentions. If that happens, he will act unpredictably, and we will have no way of knowing what he will do."

Menes and Ramses's shoulders slumped in defeat.

"What do you suggest we do then?" Menes asked with a sigh.

"We continue as normal. Only the three of us know what we believe his plan is." Menes reluctantly agreed while Ramses looked ready to argue further.

Menes saw the lost look on his son's face. He stepped forward and gently hugged Liviana. "I trust your judgment," he whispered in her ear. He pulled back and looked her in the eyes. "Talk to him." He motioned to Ramses, who sat on his throne, face in hands. "He worries about you." With a gentle pat on the shoulders, Menes left Ramses and Liviana alone.

Liviana watched Ramses for a moment before approaching. She knelt in front of him and took his hands in hers. Despite the slight resistance from Ramses, Liviana pulled his hands from his face and held them in his lap. Looking back up at his face, she noticed streaks of tears running down his reddened cheeks. Without saying a word, she raised a hand and carefully thumbed away any new tears that started to join the rest in their journey down Ramses's face.

In turn, Ramses gently grabbed the wrist of the hand on his face and gently pulled Liviana to stand.

Liviana put up no resistance and allowed her distraught husband to continue to pull her until she was sitting across his lap with his face buried in her neck. She wrapped her arms around his neck and gently ran her fingers through his hair.

They sat there, taking in the comfort the other gave, neither saying a word.

After a while, Ramses pulled back and placed a kiss on Liviana's forehead. "I still believe you should have more guards around you now," he said, looking into her eyes.

Liviana sighed. "If it were any other circumstance, or anyone else attempting something, I would agree wholeheartedly. But I have watched my brother grow into the person he is today. If he thinks he has the upper hand, he is calm and has many plans up his sleeves. But as soon as he knows someone is onto him or something unexpectedly messes up his plans, he forgets everything and takes the obstacle out without a single thought."

Ramses gave a sigh of his own and lightly pressed their foreheads together. "I say, with complete reluctance, that I understand where you are coming from. I just worry that this plan to do nothing will backfire on us."

Liviana gave it a thought before smiling. "How about a compromise?" she asked. "Whenever I am away from you or your father within the palace, I have one guard with me." She paused to give Ramses time to think. "And whenever we are away from the palace, we have one extra guard with us and two more following from a distance."

"I can agree to that," he answered. "As long as you agree that these conditions can change if the situation changes."

Liviana nodded in agreement before snuggling closer to the man she loved.

They basked in the silent presence of each other once again, both wondering what the near future would hold for them.

Chapter 14

"This isn't normal," Liviana told Ramses as they walked through the palace halls. "Something isn't right."

"What makes you say that?" Ramses inquired. He had an idea that it had something to do with Claudius, but he could not say exactly what it was.

"He isn't doing anything." She came to a stop at a nearby window and looked out to the Roman camp in the distance. "He's been out there for two months, and he hasn't made a single move against us." She leaned back against Ramses when he wrapped her in his arms. "What if we were wrong? What if it wasn't me he was waiting for?"

Ramses hummed. "I think the fact that he hasn't tried anything in two months shows that we were right. We've been very careful to make sure you are never alone and keeping to how we have always acted. Maybe he hasn't had the proper opportunity yet."

Liviana shook her head. "No. That's not it. I have watched him grow up. He has never been one for patience. I haven't seen him wait for anything for more than a month. Anything longer than that, and he throws a Royal Tantrum."

They stood in contemplative silence for a few minutes before Ramses gently guided her away from the window and back down the hall. "How are you feeling today?" he asked her quietly.

"Better than the other day."

"I still think you should go and see the physician." For the past week, Liviana hadn't been feeling well, and Ramses was starting to get worried.

Liviana stopped suddenly, forcing Ramses to turn to face her from the arm still holding her waist. "You need to forget about it," she demanded when he was looking at her face on.

Ramses frowned. "No," he denied. "I can't just forget about it. Not when I wake up to you being physically sick. Not when you are sending half a plate full of food back to the kitchens at the end of every meal. And especially not when you aren't listening to a word of concern from your own husband." By the end of his rant, Ramses had raised his voice to the point that all the servants and guards in the hall stopped to stare at the pair.

"It's like I told you," Liviana said. "The stress from the last month has finally caught up to me."

"No." Ramses turned his back on Liviana, took two steps away, then turned back to her, pointing a finger. "Stress would be one reaction or another. Not both at once."

"Who are you to tell me what stress would do to me?"

"Being the son of someone who had to raise me by himself while ruling an entire country and bringing it back to the prosperity it once had, has shown me a thing or two. I know what stress can do to a person."

"And you think I haven't?" she asked, now raising her voice to match his. "My mother was killed soon after my brother was born. So, I too, was raised by my father alone.

He refused to hand Claudius and I over to be looked after by someone else." She stepped forward to get right into Ramses's face. "Then he had to watch his own son grow into a boy who had not a care in the world for anyone other than himself. I had to hold his hand as he cried himself to sleep every night. I had to beg him to eat when he didn't have anything." She jabbed a finger into his chest. "So don't you dare tell me you have seen what stress can do!"

They both stood breathing heavily.

Ramses was the first to break the silence. "Until you are willing to listen to reason, I think it best for you to find somewhere else to sleep." He walked back two steps. "I believe the room you were given when you first arrived is still available." With his final piece said, he turned his back against her and stormed off down the hall.

Liviana gave a short, frustrated scream before turning and storming in the opposite direction of Ramses, a guard scrambling to keep her within his sight.

Unknown to the pair, their argument had been witnessed by a dozen dazed servants and guards as well as a very stunned Menes.

Chapter 15

Liviana had done what Ramses had suggested and gone to the room that she had first resided in. Being in there reminded her of a simpler time when she didn't have to worry about her life being at the hands of her scheming brother. At that moment, she felt anger for Claudius like she had never felt before, not even when she found out that he had killed their father.

The only sounds penetrating the silent room were those of Juliana making the room suitable and ready for the annoyed princess, and the guard shuffling nervously as he waited for another to join him.

Eventually, Liviana could not take the silence any longer and grabbed a bed pillow she was leaning against and screamed into it.

Juliana gave a slight giggle at the sight Liviana made, a girl in a royal dress lounging on the room's bed with a pillow over her face like a child would to hide. "Are you ready to talk now?" she asked.

Liviana sat up properly on the bed and slammed the pillow into her lap. Sighing, she waved the guard to stand outside the door. He was reluctant to, but as she was his princess, he had no choice but to obey.

Juliana waited for the door to close before going to sit beside Liviana on the bed. "I only heard from the other servants what happened," she said, grabbing one of Liviana's hands in hers. "But I want to hear it from you."

Liviana sighed again. "He wasn't listening to me when I was telling him I'm feeling ill from the stress and worrying with Claudius having caught up to me."

The girls sat in silence before Juliana timidly asked, "Could it be something else?"

Liviana shook her head. "I don't think so. My father had the same symptoms whenever he got too stressed."

"I think he's just doing his job as your husband and showing he cares about you through his own worry."

Liviana ripped her hand from Juliana's and stood up. "But he doesn't have to tell me I'm wrong." She started to pace around the room. "He can show me he cares in other ways. He can ask what's worrying me. He can suggest activities that can take my mind off of what's making me ill." She picked up a pillow from a bench she was passing. "He doesn't need to show me his care by telling me I need to see a physician and not listen when I say I'm fine, then decide to banish me from my own room when I stand up for myself." She glared at the pillow in her hands. Squeezing it tight, she gave a scream before throwing it at the door just as it opened.

The person entering the room noticed the projectile coming their way and closed the door before it hit. They slowly opened the door to check it was safe to enter and to see what had been thrown their way.

Liviana hadn't noticed she had almost hit someone in her anger, as she had turned her back to the door as soon as the pillow had left her hand. Ignoring everything going on around her, she continued to pace around the room.

"Well," the person at the door said. "I haven't had a pillow thrown at me since my Queen was pregnant with Ramses."

Liviana's eyes widened, and she spun around to face the new person in the room. She was shocked to find Menes standing in the doorway holding the pillow she had just inadvertently thrown at him. She threw her hands over her mouth in her shocked state. "I am so sorry. I hadn't known you were coming in."

Menes took another step into the room and let the door shut behind him. "Not to worry, my dear. You have every right to be throwing things around in private." He walked to Liviana and held the pillow out for her to take. She took her hands from her mouth and grabbed the pillow with a sheepish smile. "I have had plenty of pillows thrown at me throughout the years." He sat on the bench Liviana had conveniently stopped by. "At least, it wasn't a vase." She smiled back. "Those tend to hurt upon impact."

Liviana laughed. "I'm still sorry for almost hitting you. I should have paid more attention."

Menes put up his hand in a stop motion. "Say no more. You weren't expecting anyone to come through the door, were you?" Liviana shook her head. "Then you have nothing to apologize for. I should have knocked first instead of just bursting right in."

She stared down at the pillow once again in her hands. "I've just been angry since the…" She stopped not knowing if Menes had heard about her argument with Ramses.

Menes gave a soft sigh. "I know," he said.

Liviana quickly turned her head up to look at him wide-eyed. Consequently, she had to blink quickly to counteract the dizziness that overcame her.

Menes gave a small laugh. "You weren't exactly quiet about it." He paused. "I also happen to have been walking down that very hallway and stumbled on the two of you mid-argument."

Liviana closed her eyes and took a deep breath, both to show her horror and to further stave off the dizziness. It seemed that nothing she did could stop the feeling.

Menes moved from the bench and to the frozen Liviana. He placed his hands gently on her shoulders. "I know you probably don't want to hear this again, but he really does care about you, and he does not know how to show his worry to you."

The added pressure from Menes's hands, despite how gentle, was too much for Liviana's body to handle. Her legs could no longer hold her up, and she began to collapse.

"Ana," Menes yelled as he caught her and gently brought himself to kneel, holding her close to him.

She felt herself being cradled, and the last thing Liviana heard before the darkness took her was Menes calling for the guard and begging her to stay awake.

Chapter 16

Voices penetrated the darkness Liviana was floating in. She could not understand what they were saying, nor could she recognize who the voices belonged to. The darkness was pressing down on her and felt heavier on her hands and head.

Slowly, the darkness started to give way to light. The first thing she was able to properly feel was the feeling of a wet cloth on her head.

Getting more feeling, she squeezed the heaviness on her hand.

The voices stopped, and everything fell silent. Soon a rush of wind sounded, and the voices came back. Only this time, they seemed to be more concerned than before.

She squeezed the heaviness again, and once again, the voices fell silent. She expected them to start again. But the heaviness squeezed back.

Only one voice started speaking again. Liviana still could not understand what it was saying, but she could feel that it was somehow pulling her closer to the ever-so-slowly growing light.

"…Ana," she heard this voice calling when the light was surrounding her. "Can you hear me?"

She squeezed what she could now feel as a hand in hers and gave a small groan.

She felt another hand gently move to hold her cheek. "Can you open your eyes for us?" the voice asked. She did as the voice asked, only to close her eyes again when it became too bright too quickly.

"Slowly, your Highness," another voice advised.

"Juliana, close the windows," a third voice gently commanded.

"Yes, my Pharaoh," a fourth replied, followed by the sound of pieces of wood hitting each other.

"Try again, your Highness," the second voice said. "Slowly," it advised when her eyes fluttered open.

Her sight was blurry once her eyes were fully open. A golden blur filled her vision, and she blinked to clear up her vision.

"Ramses," she sighed when the image of her husband wearing his crown became clear.

Ramses gave a sigh of his own in reply. "Thank the Gods." He smiled gently down at her.

"What happened?" she asked, trying to sit up. Ramses helped her before sitting on the bed she was on and pulling her into his side. She snuggled into him, glad his earlier frustration seemed to have disappeared.

"What's the last thing you remember?" the third voice from the darkness asked.

Lifting her head from Ramses's chest, she saw she was in the physician's room with Menes, Juliana, and the Physician, Amir, standing there with concern clearly written on their faces. She thought back to before the darkness had surrounded her. "I was apologizing for throwing a pillow at you, and you were saying that I had every right to throw things in private."

Amir gave a choked cough and turned to Menes wide-eyed.

Seeing the look Amir was giving him, he coughed into his hand to attempt to hide his embarrassment. "Well, yes," he agreed. "At some point, you could not cope with the stress, and you passed out."

Liviana felt Ramses's eyes on the top of her head. She looked up at him and gave a sheepish smile. "Sorry," she apologized. The only thing Ramses did was gently shake his head and kiss the top of her own.

"So, is it all the stress that made her pass out?" Juliana asked from her spot near the last window she closed.

"Before the Princess's recollection, I would have said that it was," Amir replied.

Ramses, Liviana, and Juliana looked to Amir in confusion. Menes, though, gave a similar wide-eyed expression he had received earlier. "Are you saying-?" he started but was unable to finish his question.

"The similarity is there, my Pharaoh," Amir smirked at Menes. "I'm surprised you did not see it."

Menes glared at his physician. "I was more concerned with making sure she wasn't feeling too bad after her argument with my son in the middle of the palace hall."

The two continued to bicker while the other three watched on.

Juliana moved from the window and sat on the floor in front of Liviana and Ramses. "Any idea what they are bickering about?" she asked, leaning her head on Liviana's legs.

Any other servant would have been punished for such a personal action. Luckily Liviana had told her, in no uncertain terms, that she was to treat Liviana as a friend rather than a mistress.

"All I've been able to pick out is that there is a similarity to something in what I remember and something else," Liviana replied, still watching the bickering men in confusion.

"And that it is something that Father should have also been able to see," Ramses added, also watching the other two men in the room.

Juliana felt that there was something obvious in what Liviana remembered that triggered both Menes and Amir to have a different idea as to what ails her friend. Suddenly she remembered something that Menes had said when entering Liviana's temporary chambers. "Oh, by the Gods," she exclaimed, leaping to her feet.

The others in the room jumped at the exclamation and a brief silence fell over the room.

"What's wrong?" Menes enquired in fear. He raced over to the occupants on the bed and knelt down. He grabbed Liviana's hands in his own. "Is everything okay? Are you in pain? Do you need something to drink? To eat?"

Liviana was overwhelmed by all the sudden questions and was unable to answer any of them. She knew that Menes cared about her; however, he was showing more care than she had ever thought possible for someone who wasn't immediate family.

"Father," Ramses called to interrupt his father's ramblings. Said father then looked to his son to reprimand him for not taking proper care of his wife. "There is nothing wrong." He interrupted again before Menes could speak again. "We are just as confused by Juliana's outburst as you are."

Menes turned to ask Juliana about her exclamation only to find her rummaging through Amir's cabinets, looking for something and muttering to herself.

"What are you searching for?" Amir asked only for Juliana to ignore him and continue her rummaging.

They all resigned themselves to watching Juliana without speaking another word to her.

Looking on the shelves beside the door, Juliana gave a shout of triumph and turned around, holding a jar of wheat and barley seeds mixed together. She then went over to a pile of dishes and poured a small handful of seeds onto it. Once the jar was returned to its original spot, Juliana held the dish out to Liviana. "I think you know what you need to do," she said, being vague to reduce her friend's embarrassment.

"How are seeds supposed to let us know what's got Father and Amir bickering like children?" Ramses asked in confusion upon seeing Liviana's face turning red.

"It's up to Her Highness if she wishes to tell you," Amir replied, ignoring the 'children' half of the question. "But seeing her red face, I don't think that's going to happen any time soon." Liviana shook her head, taking the dish from Juliana. "Keep it up for a week and rest as much as possible. I do not want you to stress yourself any more than you already have."

Liviana nodded and made as fast a getaway as she could on her shaking legs.

A week later, they all gathered back in the physician's room, circling a table with the dish of wheat and barley seeds laying on it. The dish was covered with a light cloth Liviana had pinched from breakfast that morning. There were lumps under the cloth where Ramses knew there shouldn't have been.

"It is obvious what the results are for those who know what this was for," Amir said with a smile. "Let's show everyone else though, shall we?"

Liviana nodded with a smile of her own and lifted the cloth from the dish.

Before all their eyes, some of the seeds had sprouted and started growing.

Ramses raised an eyebrow. "She watered some seeds that have started to grow. This tells us what exactly?"

The reactions his question got were varied. Menes coughed into his hand to hide his laugh. Juliana didn't hide her amusement and laughed. Liviana's face went as red as it did one week earlier.

Amir, on the other hand, stayed blank-faced and replied. "It tells us that you, Prince Ramses, are quite the competent husband and can satisfy your wife."

Liviana went even more red, Juliana laughed harder, and Menes could not hold his laughter any longer.

"To put it simply, your Highness, you are to be a father yourself and have provided an heir to the throne."

"But how can you tell?" he asked, still confused. "All we have to go by is a bunch of seeds Ana's watered for a week that have started to grow."

Liviana, still with a red face, patted Ramses on the arm. "I'll tell you exactly how he knows back in our chambers," she informed him.

The occupants of the room didn't realize that the door had been left slightly open, and anyone outside the door had heard everything that was going on in the room.

As such, they did not know about the two guards who had very different thoughts on the 'meant to be' private conversation.

One guard had been with Liviana from the moment she had entered the palace. He was wondering how he could spread the news without anyone being able to trace it back to him.

The other guard was new to the position. He was wondering when he would be able to get away from the palace unnoticed and report his findings back to the man who truly had his loyalty.

Chapter 17

Being a new recruit, the guard did not have to wait long at all to be able to get away and report. Claudius knew by that same evening that his sister was with child, and his claim to the throne of the Roman Empire was moving further from his grasp.

Smashes and frustrated yells were all that could be heard throughout the Roman encampment. All knew that Claudius was not happy about something he had been told. There would be no calming him down from this, and his plans to slowly draw his sister out would have to be sped up.

In his tent, Claudius was throwing anything he could get his hands on.

"First, they do not heed my request and place her in their cells," he yelled, throwing an already half-broken vase. "Then that blasted Pharaoh has the audacity to pardon my perfect sister with a law I doubt even exists." He picked up his sword and swung it into the pole which was holding his tent up. "And now I find out she's carrying the heir to the throne." He grabbed the edge of the table in his tent and flipped it over, spilling its contents all across the ground. "This was not how any of this was supposed to play out." He pulled his sword from the pole and swung it around, emphasizing some of his words. "I'm supposed to be the only heir to the throne."

He pushed his sword into the sand beneath his feet, knelt down, and placed his forehead on his hands. He stayed there breathing heavily.

Finally, he slowly looked up, a dark look crossing his face. "There is only one solution to this problem," he proclaimed to himself. "Her Royal Highness, Princess Liviana, must be eliminated."

An evil laugh was released and echoed from within the tent, throughout the Roman camp, and toward the palace. All who heard it knew that things were about to become dangerous.

Chapter 18

A week later, saw Liviana getting ready for a day wandering through the village and market.

"I know it's not my place to say anything," Juliana said, helping Liviana put her crown on her head in a way that it partially blended into her hair. "But I do not feel comfortable with you going out today with only two guards escorting you."

"Juliana," Liviana sighed with a smile.

"We all heard that sinister laughter." Juliana interrupted before Liviana could say anything further. "I know you are not concerned, but I really wish you would reconsider your escort numbers." Juliana finished putting the crown in place and moved to stand in front of her friend. "It's not only you that you have to think about now."

Liviana kept the smile on her face and gathered Juliana's hands in her own. "I am well aware that it's not only my life I have to look after now." She led Juliana to the bench near the balcony overlooking the market. "And who said anything about me not being concerned?"

Juliana laid her head on Liviana's shoulder and wrapped her arms around Liviana's waist. "You've been so calm at court sessions. And you haven't once mentioned your brother since you found out you were pregnant."

Liviana laughed, placing her head atop of Juliana's and wrapping her up in her arms. "I've been trying not to stress too much, so I've been avoiding activities and conversations that cause stress." She hugged Juliana tighter. "That's not to say that I haven't been stressing. It's just been in the privacy of my own chambers with Ramses there to calm me down."

"I still don't feel comfortable with you going out there until everything is settled and he leaves."

"He may never leave." Liviana sighed. "With Claudius, things are not settled until he gets what he wants." She moved her head to look down at Juliana. "As for not going out. I will not be stuck hiding in the palace making the people believe that we do not care about them or to make them feel that we are above them in any way."

Juliana lifted her head off Liviana's shoulder to look up at her. "But Ana, two guards might not be enough to keep you safe out there."

"Which is why," Ramses said, appearing at the door, "there will be more guards following them dressed as people attending to their normal daily tasks." The girls watched Ramses cross the room and sit on the other side of Liviana to Juliana. "We've had it planned for a couple of days now."

Juliana frowned, wondering why she didn't know about this plan. They had never kept anything from her before this.

As if she had read Juliana's mind, Liviana hugged her closer again. "You had a day off when it was decided we finally needed to do something to draw him out," she said.

"Father then declared that anyone who did not need to know was not to be told," Ramses continued.

"We felt the laughter we heard was Claudius finding out about the baby."

"The only ones who knew were those in the physician's chambers and possibly the two guards posted outside the door."

"We knew the ones inside the room would not have said anything, so that only leaves the guards at the door."

Juliana's head moved from side to side throughout the dual explanation before settling on Liviana when she finished. "So, to prove this theory of yours, only the royals and guards were told the plan?"

"Yes," Liviana confirmed.

"Not even the advisers knew," Ramses also confirmed. "They are all of the belief that Ana and I have been ordered by Father and Amir to spend the day relaxing together. That means no meetings for us today."

Juliana frowned again. "But how will you get out without anyone seeing you?" she asked. "What happens if someone needs to see you at any point and you aren't here when they enter the chambers?"

"I'll sneak out through the servant's entrance in a cloak covering my clothes and hair," Liviana told her.

"And two of Father's longest serving guards will be standing outside the door with orders that only yourself and Father have permission to come and go as you please."

"It's really cute how the two of you can suddenly continue an explanation after one sentence each," Juliana declared. "But it's also really annoying."

The three laughed, enjoying their time together until Liviana decided that it was time for her to go.

Chapter 19

The plan had worked better than Liviana thought it would have. Despite the cloak hiding who she was, she expected one of the servants in the kitchen to notice when three people they did not know walked through their work area.

Yet here she was with the sun directly above, while it was just past breakfast when she left, and none of the advisers had come looking for her demanding answers as to why they had been lied to about her whereabouts. But there had also been no suspicious activity from anyone in the market.

She was starting to wonder if there really was a traitor amongst the guards. If that was the case, she did not want to even think about which of the four others in the room had betrayed her and had been lying to her face about everything. She sighed, causing her two guards to look at her suddenly.

"Is everything alright, your Highness?" one asked worriedly.

"We can take you back to the palace whenever you please," the other suggested.

"No, I'm alright," Liviana soothed. "Just overthinking things." She looked at the sun high above, then around the market. She smiled at the two of them. "I'm starting to get hungry and wish to try some food served here in the market. What would you suggest?"

The two grinned at each other then proceeded to guide Liviana to what they described as the best market food to be bought.

As the stall came into sight, they pointed it out to Liviana and enthusiastically described all the different foods that could be purchased there.

No sooner than they had pointed out the stall, that one had an arrow sticking from his shoulder, and the other had covered her with his own body to protect her from any more attacks.

"We need to get you out of here, Princess," he noted before pushing her through the growing crowd and toward an alley between stalls.

"But what about – " Liviana started, worried about the other guard who had not followed.

"He'll be fine," he reassured her before whispering in her ear. "Don't forget the hidden guards. They'll make sure he gets the help he needs." They exited onto a quiet street, and the guard raised his voice to normal. "My job is to get you back to the safety of the palace."

"Right." She nodded and allowed herself to be quickly pushed toward home.

They hadn't made it very far before someone stepped out from another alley halting their progress. He wore the clothes of the palace guard. The only difference between him and the guard who had stepped in front of her, sword drawn, was the bow he held and the quiver of arrows across his back.

Having gotten to know how the guards worked over the previous two months taught Liviana that the only time bows and arrows were to be carried was when they had left the town and trekked deep into the desert.

"I'm afraid you aren't taking her to the safety of anywhere," the guard stopping them declared.

"What are you doing?" the guard protecting her asked, confused. "We have our orders to escort the Princess back to the palace in the event of an attack."

"I have my own orders to carry out." He pulled an arrow from the quiver, placed it in the bow, and aimed it at the guard and the royal standing in front of him. "If you are going to stand in my way, I'm going to have to take you out too."

"Then bring it on." The one guarding Liviana widened his stance, getting ready to attack.

The movement caused the sun to glint from a piece of metal at the guard's waist. The glint caught Liviana's attention, and an idea came to her. She carefully pulled the metal from the waist, revealing a short dagger. If the guard noticed her theft, he did not make a move to show it. She looked around the guard's shoulder and watched the movements of the archer.

When he pulled the string of the bow taut, she took her chance to push the guard out of the way and throw the dagger at the archer.

Chapter 20

That evening Menes had called a council of advisers.

When the advisers heard what had transpired that afternoon, they were furious; none more furious than the vizier. The problem was that they weren't furious at what happened. They were angry at the fact that they had not been informed about the plan before it was to be executed.

"This goes beyond any laws of our land," the vizier announced to the entire room.

"And what laws would they be?" Ramses asked, holding a shaking Liviana. "It has always been that the Pharaoh can act without the consent of the advisers when the safety of his people is in question."

The vizier glared at his Prince. "That is true, yes," he agreed. "However, the safety of his people is not a concern at the present moment." Ramses and Menes glanced at each other, not liking where the vizier was going with his argument. "There were no signs that anyone within our city was in any danger. What this new Princess has manipulated you into doing is put our people in a position of being injured in the crossfire that Egypt has no part to play in." By the end of his argument, the vizier had closed his eyes and stuck his nose in the air in a show of smugness and arrogance.

This action caused him to fail to notice the reactions of the others in the room. The other advisers stared at him in horror, wondering what he was thinking. Ramses and Menes were outright glaring, wishing they could grab one of the guard's swords to run him through without having any backlash.

Liviana, though, had listened to his every word and realized that what he was saying was true. Claudius hadn't instigated any attacks within the city walls until that afternoon. If the archer had missed his targeted guard, he could have hit one of the people near them while minding their own business. Because of her, one of the guards was injured, and the other had come close to it if she hadn't thought so quickly. She couldn't handle her grief any longer and began to cry into Ramses, not caring about her audience.

Seeing his wife driven to tears, Ramses glared at the vizier harder, wishing his glare alone would kill the man in front of him. He opened his mouth to berate the clearly incompetent vizier.

"Get out." A voice calmly interrupted him. All eyes slowly moved to the enraged Menes. Though his words were calm, his expression was truly murderous.

The vizier, on the other hand, quickly brought his head down to look at Menes. "Excuse me?" he asked, shocked.

"You heard me quite clearly. Get out."

He tried to argue. "But my Pharaoh – "

Menes leapt up from his throne. "How dare you question me," he bellowed. Everyone's eyes widened in shock. None had ever seen Menes as enraged as he was then.

"By insinuating that Princess Liviana is nothing more than a manipulating outsider, you have insinuated that I have been blindsided in my affections for a girl I see as my daughter. By saying that none of my people have been in danger before this afternoon, you are implying that Princess Liviana is not one of my people. As such, you have insulted your Princess and, by extension, the royal family." Menes moved to stand in front of the frozen vizier. "Now, I will not say it again. Get out. And do not come to me with anything until I personally call for you."

As he did one month prior, the vizier gave a non-verbal reply, this time as a nod, and rushed from the room before anything else could be said.

Silence reigned once the doors had closed.

"Who could have organized something like this?" one of the remaining advisers asked. "It was clear that their target was Princess Liviana. But the people love her."

The advisers murmured in agreement.

"It was Claudius," Liviana announced, and all eyes turned to her. "He has finally decided to make a move against me."

"If you don't mind me asking, Princess," the same adviser began. "How do you know it's him?"

Liviana pulled away from Ramses and looked to the advisers. "Do we still have the arrows the archer used?" They nodded and motioned for one of the guards to bring the quiver forward. She pulled out one arrow and looked at the head of it. "This is why," she said, pointing to the head. "Roman arrowheads are made from bronze and have a sharp tip. Your arrowheads, however, are made of stone and have a more rounded shape."

Sure enough, the arrow in Liviana's hand had a bronze pointed tip.

"We have to go and confront him about this," another adviser demanded.

"Unfortunately, that's not going to work."

"But why not, Princess?" the third and final adviser asked. "We have proof that he sent someone to either kidnap or kill you."

"We may have proof and know it was him, yes. But until we catch him with the weapons aimed at me himself, he will continue to place the blame on someone else. That's exactly what he did back home and now look where we are."

They all fell silent in hesitant acceptance.

Menes was the first to break the silence. "Until such an event occurs, we have to be more vigilant wherever you go," he commanded. "Even within the palace." Everyone in the room nodded in agreement, and Menes dismissed them all. When Liviana was at the door, he complimented her. "Nice aim with that dagger, my dear. Whoever your tutor was would be proud of you."

She smiled sadly. "It was all luck," she replied. "That was the first time I had ever thrown a blade of any type."

She turned around and walked out the door with two guards following, leaving behind an astounded Ramses and Menes.

Chapter 21

"That soldier was useless," Claudius seethed. "He couldn't even carry out a simple kidnapping." He paced around his tent. "I have one other plan I could use before going myself. But I have to wait."

"Forgive me for interrupting Emperor," a centurion spoke, bowing just inside the tent's entrance.

"What is it?" Claudius snapped. "You know not to interrupt me when I'm planning."

"I apologize, Emperor. But you asked to be informed when that package you asked for arrived."

Claudius smirked darkly. "Perfect timing."

Sneaking into the palace kitchens that evening, and finding a servant who could do his bidding, was easier than Claudius thought it would be. All he had to do was dress as an Egyptian commoner and look like he knew what he was doing.

"I really have to get back to the kitchens," the servant said after Claudius had dragged her away. "Dinner is about to start, and I have to make sure to get the plates to the Pharaoh and his family quickly."

"You will," he soothed. "I just need to give you these." He pulled a few candles from the pouch at his waist. "I heard that the Princess has been stressed lately. Lighting these will help her to sleep easier and wake up less stressed."

The servant took the candles from him. "I'll see what I can do. Thank you." She nodded to him and made her way back to the kitchens.

The dark smirk crossed Claudius's face again as he watched the servant walk away. "That's all I need you to do. After all, how can anyone say no to something that is beneficial for their princess? And once everyone's fallen asleep while eating, I can go in there and end my wretched sister. Baby and all."

Chapter 22

Dinner that night had a different feel to it than any other over the previous couple of months. There didn't seem to be anything different as they all sat down to eat. The candles burned gently on the table, the torches cast their glow from the walls, and the kitchen staff stood ready to put their plates in front of them. Despite all the similarities to any other nightly meal, the air had a calmer feel to it than at any other time.

The same people were in attendance as was usual since they had all found out that Liviana was with child. Menes sat at the head of the table. Ramses sat to his father's left with Liviana beside him. Amir sat opposite Ramses with Juliana beside him, opposite Liviana.

That night, Liviana was feeling playful and would throw her berries at Juliana whenever she wasn't looking.

"That's it," Juliana snapped after the fourth piece of fruit hit her. She turned to Ramses and Liviana with a glare. "I don't know which one of you it is, but it stopped being funny after the first two hits."

"What are you talking about?" Ramses asked incredulously. "We haven't been hitting you with anything."

Liviana nodded her head in agreement with a look of concern on her face.

"Then how do you explain the extra fruit that has mysteriously appeared on my plate?"

Ramses and Liviana shrugged their shoulders in confusion, fake confusion in Liviana's case.

Menes, who had seen what Liviana was doing from the beginning, decided to play along with the mischief. "Perhaps the cook simply put more fruit on your plate by accident," he offered. "Or you were given the wrong plate and had not noticed."

"But – " Juliana started before realizing she had lost the argument before it really began. "Fine." She sighed in defeat before pointing at Ramses and Liviana. "This isn't over. I will find out the truth."

The conversations began to flow as they had before Juliana had enough of being the target of food.

It was when their dessert, honey cakes, had been served that Amir noticed that something wasn't feeling right. He looked around the table and noticed that everyone's eyes were starting to close, and they were all falling asleep where they sat. Frowning, he closed his eyes and concentrated on the evening. The food tasted as it always did, so there was nothing wrong there. It could not have been their drinks causing them to fall asleep. The men had wine while the women had water. So, unless whatever it was, was put into their cups individually, it wasn't administered that way. Taking in a deep breath to help the thinking process, he caught the scent of something that did not belong in the banquet room. Opening his eyes, he found that the scent was coming from the candles sitting innocently in the middle of the table.

"Princess Liviana," he called, standing up. When he was sure he had the attention of everyone in the room, he continued. "I am aware that it is late, but I feel that I need to check on your health."

"Can't it wait until the morning, Amir?" Menes asked on behalf of the sleepy princess. "We're all tired, and I'm sure we would all appreciate going to bed without any worries."

"Unfortunately, not my Pharaoh. This *must* be done immediately. Physician's orders, I'm afraid."

The occupants of the table let out soft groans before begrudgingly following Amir to his chambers.

"What is the meaning of this, Amir?" Menes demanded once they were in the healing chambers.

He was standing, leaning on the wall near the door, trying to fight off sleep. Juliana was curled up on one of the seats in the room, close to sleep. Ramses was sat on the bed, his head bobbing in an effort to stave off sleep. Liviana was laid on the bed, her head in Ramses's lap, as close to sleep as Juliana was. Amir was the only one who was not affected by sleep as he was rummaging through one of his many cupboards.

"Do not fall asleep," he commanded sharply. Liviana and Juliana's closed eyes snapped open, and Ramses sat up straighter.

Eventually, Amir found what he was looking for and turned to face those in the room. He was holding what could only be described as a bulked root of a plant. He went to a bench and started to chop and grind the root.

"Amir, I command you to tell me what is going on," Menes said in his Pharaoh voice. "Why have you demanded to check on Liviana tonight instead of waiting until the morning?"

"With respect, my Pharaoh," Amir said with his back still facing the room. "I'm not going to explain everything until I know you are all wide awake."

Menes gave an unsightly huff and continued to stand, waiting in frustrated silence.

The other three waited in confused silence, trying to abide by Amir's command to not fall asleep.

When Amir turned around again, he was holding a small plate, with the root ground into a paste and a spoon. He went around the room, telling each occupant to take a small amount and eat it.

They all had the same reaction when placing the paste in their mouths. They screwed their faces up at the extremely bitter taste. But it did its expected job, and they became wide awake again.

"*Now,* will you tell us why you have brought us here?" Menes asked Amir with an eyebrow raised.

"Of course," he answered with a nod. He faced Liviana. "I believe with his failed attempt on you two days ago; your brother made another attempt against you tonight."

Liviana's eyes widened, and she sat up on the bed from her position laying in Ramses's lap.

"But how do you know?" Ramses asked. "No one came near us all night except to serve our food or to fill our cups. And none of them made any moves against us."

Liviana frowned. "He does not always go for the obvious nor the violent," she commented. "He can be subtle when he needs to be."

"And this time, he did use a subtle means," Amir agreed. "Didn't you find it coincidental that all of you started to fall asleep at exactly the same time?"

They all shook their heads.

"How could he have done that?" Juliana asked. "The food didn't taste any different, and we all drank at different paces and times."

"It was the candles on the table. They were scented with the same oil we use in our mummification process. The workers can fall asleep where they stand if they are not used to the effects."

"Lavender," Juliana whispered. "It's used quite commonly in Rome."

"It's true," Liviana agreed. "We use it in our cooking and baths. It is well known that high exposure to the oil can cause someone to sleep for hours, and nothing can wake them."

"Right," Menes said after a moment of silence. "He's tried an obvious attempt and now a subtle attempt. What do you think his next move will be, Ana?"

Liviana sighed. "As much as he won't want to, with two failed attempts, he might come for me himself. Most likely during the night while everyone in the palace is asleep."

"In that case, I'll have guards posted at all possible entry points to your chambers until further notice," Menes decided.

"It won't take him long. We've really backed him into a corner here."

"Can I suggest that the ones on the balcony aren't in obvious sight," Ramses recommended. "Obviously, make sure they can see if someone comes in, but make sure they themselves aren't seen. We want him to think he's going to get away with his plan."

Menes agreed, and they planned throughout the night until they fell asleep in various places around the room.

Chapter 23

"This is unbelievable," Claudius ranted within his tent the next day. "This is the third plan of mine they have thwarted." He paced around the tent, still ranting. "First, I can't get her because of her preposterous marriage to that pompous prince. *Then* she has to go and provide an heir, so they increase the guard. That stupid spy has to then go ahead and fail at kidnapping her. Failing that, he couldn't even manage to get rid of her to hide my involvement. And *finally,* that ridiculous healer then went and noticed what was happening at the table and smelled the candles."

He gave a loud cry of frustration then proceeded to destroy anything in his tent that had escaped the previous destruction until nothing was left in one piece.

"There isn't anything I can give to anyone else to handle. There isn't anything else I can plan to fulfill my ambition of being an only child."

Sunlight glinting off something in the sand caught his attention. Slowly he bent to pick up the object. A smirk very quickly crossed his face.

"Or maybe there is. Wouldn't it be brilliant if I dispose of my only two obstacles in the same way?"

He let out an insane laugh, for in his hand was the same dagger he used to kill his father and frame his sister.

The guards around the camp knew that anyone who was heard making even a little bit of noise would not be seen alive again. So, they all made sure not to get too close to Claudius's tent and to not speak any louder than a whisper.

Chapter 24

He didn't take long to implement his last plan. He knew this would be his last plan, and it would spell doom for one of the Roman siblings. He was confident that it wouldn't be himself.

For three days, Claudius familiarized himself with how the palace ran and which room would inevitably be the place where his sister would breathe her last. He now knew that, wherever she went, Liviana had an escort of four people – two guards and a combination of the prince, the Pharaoh, the healer or the slave.

He knew that the only time to execute his plan was deep into the night after everyone had gone to bed. They had stationed two guards to stand outside their chamber doors. However, they had left their balcony entirely exposed and unguarded.

So, on the fourth night, he dressed in dark clothes, grabbed his dagger, and silently made his way to the palace. He found himself some luck in that those in charge of the palace gardens had planted a vine under his intended balcony and that it had grown high and sturdy enough for him to climb.

Pulling himself onto the balcony, Claudius caught sight of his prey sleeping soundly in her bed. Sneaking closer, he saw she was cuddled up next to her precious prince. Making a quick adjustment to the plan, Claudius knew he also had to dispose of the prince who had made him so desperate in his actions.

Fixated on his target and making his way further into the room, Claudius failed to notice that the two hidden guards had spotted him and were following his every step with silent ones of their own.

Reaching the side of the bed Liviana lay on he stopped and stared. Finally, he spoke, his voice echoing throughout the otherwise silent room. "This wouldn't have happened if you weren't so damned observant," he said. "If you and Father hadn't noticed how my words and actions contradicted the way I showed myself to our people, I would have been happy to wait for my turn on the throne. But you did notice. And Father chose you to be his successor. So, he had to go. Naturally, you also had to go so I could rule. But you escaped, and it has been hell getting to this point." He pulled the dagger from its scabbard at his waist and held it high above his head. "Now it's your turn to join Father in the Underworld."

As he started to bring the dagger down, he was grabbed from behind. One person pulled him away from the bed while another grabbed the hand holding the dagger and pulled it free.

He thrashed against the hold. "I demand you let me go," he yelled. "Do you have any idea who I am?"

The commotion he was making woke the occupants of the bed and alerted the guards outside the door to the danger.

They ran into the room as Claudius continued his loud ranting.

"You should never have been born," he yelled at Liviana, curled up to Ramses. "I should have been the first and only born child of Emperor Antonius. You and Father brought this upon yourselves."

Ramses held a trembling Liviana closer as he addressed the four guards in the room. "I have had enough of this," he said crossly. "Take him to the dungeons, and do not let him out of your sight."

"Yes, my Prince," all four answered simultaneously and proceeded to drag Claudius out, kicking and screaming.

He continued to make a fuss all the way to the dungeons waking any and all occupants of the rooms he passed.

By the time Ra had risen the next day, everyone was well aware that Claudius had been taken into custody and would be sentenced for punishment that very day.

Chapter 25

That day, as soon as breakfast had been eaten, the royal family made their way to the throne room for the sentencing of Claudius. When they arrived, they were surprised by the number of people who had taken time out of their day to come and watch the proceedings; it seemed as though all the staff within the palace as well as all the villagers had come and gathered as close together as possible so that as many as possible could be crammed in.

Once Menes, Ramses, and Liviana had taken their seats, Claudius was dragged in.

He started to rant as soon as he was forced to kneel and had spotted Liviana sitting on her throne. No questions needed to be asked at any time. Claudius had spilled everything before the sentencing had even begun. He confessed to the murder of his father in such a way that only Liviana could get the blame for it. He confessed to having one of his people pose as a royal guard and attempt to kidnap or murder Liviana. He spoke of how he posed as one of the palace staff and gave the candles to one of the kitchen staff so he could kill her himself. Finally, he confessed to deciding to end her himself with the same dagger he used on their father and deciding at the last moment to end Ramses along with Liviana.

With his confession to murder and attempted murder freely given, Claudius was seen as guilty and sentenced to death by pike.

From that day on, Rome and Egypt were ruled as one, with an adviser ruling Rome under direct orders from Liviana.

As for Liviana, she stayed happily married to Ramses and ruled by his side when Menes passed. They had two sons together, both being heirs to a kingdom. Their eldest became the heir to Egypt. The younger of the two became the heir of Rome and moved to his mother's homeland once he was old enough to rule in her stead.

All was peaceful across the two great nations.

However, as history goes on, conflicts arise. And the cycle of war, peace, and revolution will continue forever.

CPSIA information can be obtained
at www.ICGtesting.com
Printed in the USA
LVHW011040170523
747209LV00007B/433